Dielle Ciesco has magically tapped into the sacred shamanic voice that resides deep in the heart of all creation. Matrina, the Unknown Mother, reminds us that sound and words have the power to heal what ails humanity when we are willing to surrender to the Great Mystery. As the creator of Shamanic Breathwork Journeys, I believe that Matrina must have been whispering her wisdom in my ears these many years while I slept!

Linda Star Wolf, Author of *Shamanic Breathwork: Journeying Beyond the Limits of the Self* and *Visionary Shamanism: Activating the Imaginal Cells of the Human Energy Field*

In The Unknown Mother, author Dielle Ciesco has drawn together insightful wisdom, practical exercises, and powerful realizations of many of the greater understandings of all that sound is and can be, in a most creative approach. Through the eyes of a student, in a playful novel form, she incorporates the experienced discernment of an other-worldly teacher, offering penetrating messages on the power of the spoken word, the use of voice and intention in singing, mantra & toning, and the clarity that arises through silence, offering real life application to this most expansive body of knowledge, reaching toward one's authentic being and potential.

Zacciah Blackburn, PhD Director, the Center of Light Institute of Sound Healing and Shamanic Studies Director of Education, the International Sound Healing Network

The Unknown Mother is a must-read for anyone looking to deepen their connection to their authentic voice and tune to their inner vibration. Dielle beautifully shares powerful teachings in a lighthearted, fun manner that will effortlessly guide you into a brand new relationship with sound, love, and your own freedom.

Heather Ash Amara, Author of *The Toltec Path of Transformation*

Truly, I have not read such a well-timed and inspirational message in a long time. At the juncture of quantum reconstruction and nuclear annihilation, mankind may be ready to rewrite the chronicle of this present dysfunctional civilization. If you are ready for the next level, read this book. The Unknown Mother within you is waiting for your commands. She wants to coach you and teach you how to positively bring into play the power to speak in a new healing language. By the power of sound and speech, we can turn today's tragic failures into a new triumphant reality.

Modify your vocabulary and you revolutionize your destiny. Alter the way you string together yours words and you automatically renovate the sense of your personal history. Be aware of the supernatural properties of the words you use constantly and you gradually free yourself from the psychological dungeon of your own script. Learn how to really breathe again in harmony with the shamanic music of your universal life. The Unknown Mother is not only a wonderful Goddess of Sound; she is also a spiritual healer who knows the art of cleansing and purifying all distressing residues stuck within the cells of our body.

Immersed in this spellbinding story, the reader will be impressed by Ciesco's knowledge about the hidden force of her or his own human voice. I myself was fascinated to read about how my repressed emotions have a profound impact on my ability to express myself and adjust my entire life. Ciesco writes about some real universal solutions: learning to truly communicate and listen to others; transcending judgment with discernment; becoming our own healer; freeing our subconscious from traumatic emotions; and, more important, coming to a much deeper acceptance of what is here and now. At the end of the story, we harness the capacity to create what comes next. Being a victim is not an option anymore.

Patrick Barnard, Author of *Music As Yoga: Discover the Healing Power of Sound*

In *The Unknown Mother*, Dielle takes us on a journey into the magical world of sound through the power of story. She makes this unseen world accessible by weaving together elements both imagined and real, and gives us tools for going deeper into its mysteries. This book is helping me in my own work as a singer-songwriter, and as an herbalist who hears the voices of the plant devas. We will all be empowered to raise our voices in a new song for a new earth through Dielle's unveiling of the frequencies of The Unknown Mother, who literally creates our world.

Thea Summer Deer, PhD, Author of *Wisdom of the Plant Devas: Herbal Medicine for a New Earth*

Refreshingly deep and harmonically sweet.

Francis Rico, Author of *A Shaman's Guide to Deep Beauty: Connecting with the Mojo of the Universe*

The Unknown Mother

A Magical Walk with the
Goddess of Sound

The Unknown Mother

A Magical Walk with the
Goddess of Sound

Dielle Ciesco

Winchester, UK
Washington, USA

First published by Roundfire Books, 2013
Roundfire Books is an imprint of John Hunt Publishing Ltd., Laurel House, Station Approach,
Alresford, Hants, SO24 9JH, UK
office1@jhpbooks.net
www.johnhuntpublishing.com
www.roundfire-books.com

For distributor details and how to order please visit the 'Ordering' section on our website.

Text copyright: Dielle Ciesco 2012

ISBN: 978 1 78099 631 8

A CIP catalogue record for this book is available from the British Library.

Design: Stuart Davies

Printed and bound by CPI Group (UK) Ltd, Croydon, CR0 4YY

We operate a distinctive and ethical publishing philosophy in all
areas of our business, from our global network of authors to
production and worldwide distribution.

CONTENTS

This book is dedicated to
my teachers
past, present, and future
(that should cover everyone)
with great love and gratitude
and to the beautiful tree
upon which this book is written
(or which was spared if this is digital)

Foreword

I have read what seem like a million self-help, religious, biographical, philosophical, and metaphysical books, not to mention stacks of fiction. So what is it that I have to say that hasn't already been said in so many ways? If I take away the cover, the title, and the author from any book, and if I disregard the way in which the story is told, I basically have the same story...Love. When I glance at my bookshelf, I realize that I have somehow purchased the same book over and over again. I have been giving my short-term memory the same message, but forgetting each time.

I have read some wonderful books! They have indeed had an impact on my life, some for the here-and-now and others for much longer, affecting me more deeply. Some I have been reading over and over for years now, while I have another that has taken me six years to read through once! I sometimes check something out from the library only to realize I've already read it.

It seems there are many flavors of Love. Rather than fully grasp the meaning once and for all, I search for it yet again in a different color jacket, a different practice, or in different wording...an endless quest to one-up myself. The message is always the same no matter the messenger or the vehicle of the message. And while each path is clothed in a different cover with a different title, the message remains...Love. There is nothing else.

I hope you enjoy this version of it.

Acknowledgments

I wish to first express my gratitude to an amazing dreamer and healer, Gene Nathan, for his integrity, patience, and love as I ever so slowly relearned how to dream over my years in working with him. Thanks for letting me soak your good sweaters with my tears. It is my pleasure to love you; to my gifted editor Mark Bloom, who ironically is the spittin' image of Gene Nathan; to Dottie Baker for her catalyzing reminder that I said I wanted to write; and to Alexa Ingersoll, without whom I never would have organized this information in my head; and to all my clients who amaze me again and again with their courage.

I would also like to acknowledge the many other teachers I've worked with, whether in person or through their written works over the years; The Toltecs: don Miguel Ruiz, Raven Smith and HeatherAsh Amara, Gini Gentry, Francis Rico, Alan Hardman, Oksana Yufa, and Gary Van Warmerdam; and the Sound and Breath Folks: Mitch Nur and Two Horses Running, Hazrat Inayat Khan, Ted Andrews, Laurel Elizabeth Keyes, Don Campbell, Lama Khyimsar Rinpoche, Joseph Rael, Paul Newham, Patrick Bernard, Jonathan Goldman, Arthur Samuel Joseph, John Beaulieu, Carola Speads, and Joy Gardner. Each of you has inspired me in so many ways.

Special thanks to Marco Noto for telling me to read *The Music Lesson*, hence giving me the lightbulb moment to write fiction, and to Victor for writing the book; to JoAnn and Gary Chambers for so many opportunities to create, for your music and friendship; to Thea Summer Deer, Linda Star Wolf, and Zacchia Blackburn for your belief in this book; and to each of my friends and colleagues who read this text at different stages offering their suggestions and encouragement.

And finally, to my parents, Pat and Frank, and to Wendy, Lynn, Mark and Diane, my family.

And to all the people I may have forgotten to mention who have had a hand in the creation of this book directly or indirectly, I thank you.

PART I

SOUL SONG

Tonight I shut my eyes
    and went mute
        away
            into the arms of my Beloved

Tomorrow when I wake
    I will not be this me
        but
            the blissful embodiment of love me

It is I who must encourage the growth
    of the seeds of my desires
        as
            He plants them in my depths

With a free will
    I will sing my soul's song
        bright and clear
            throat wide, arms open

First Encounter

One night, I stopped believing in God. Well, my idea of God anyway. Like most people, I had this concept of a Supreme Being hanging out in the clouds watching everything I did, either smiling down and showering me with rewards or shaking his finger at me and withholding. For the greater part of my life, I've been looking for signs from God. I'd waited for God to rescue me in the midst of bad decisions. I'd waited for God to tell me what to do. I'd waited for God to change my life. Of course, that never happened.

My life was nothing like what I'd expected or dreamed. Instead, it was confusing and empty, full of unfulfilled dreams, unrealized talents, and desperate longings. I thought of myself as a female Salieri, the envious composer of mediocrity depicted in the movie *Amadeus*. It seemed that God had given me talent with no substance…just enough creativity to elicit tantalizing praise that never satisfied, just enough half-baked ideas that never grew wings, and just enough drive to keep me forever spinning my creative wheels. Little wonder I never accomplished anything or felt satisfied…I had projected all my power to choose and to create onto my faulty image of God.

I admit I was devastated by my crisis in faith at first. I felt frightened and alone. I felt abandoned. I couldn't believe that I, such a spiritual person, would ever, ever stop believing in God. The thing is, when I stopped believing in the idea of a God who seemed to have an investment in keeping me miserable, I freed myself to take responsibility for my own life. I assure you, it was quite a revelation.

I saw how I blamed God in all those moments He failed to

stop me from doing something stupid. I realized with no small amount of grief that it was in my power to stop myself all along. I was waiting for a sign from God, while shirking responsibility and forgetting that that sign was me! Had I just tuned into my ironically God-given body, thoughts, and intuition, I could be living a different, less stressful life.

When I stopped believing in my faulty concept of God as rescuer and God as authority, I began to understand God as something much different: an impersonal cosmic force. God wasn't a man with a white beard (or a woman with an ivory mane) withholding love and approval or handing down punishments for all my faults. I began to understand God as a frequency, a universal law more closely defined as "cause and effect."

Feeling sorry for myself wasn't getting me anywhere. I had become so weary of the handed-down image of what God was supposed to be. I was tired of my own image of what *I* was supposed to be. When I released these notions, I finally sank to my knees in surrender without the baggage of spiritual dogma. My head was completely clear. That's when it happened.

ꙮ

I lit a candle and sat in front of my mirror. I'd done this before as a way to be present with myself. As usual, in the semi-darkness, my reflection began to flicker and morph, sometimes disappearing from view altogether as the candle flame danced and sputtered. I began breathing very rhythmically, gazing deeply into and beyond the image of myself. All of the sudden, a woman's face appeared. This wasn't just my face shifting in the darkness; it was somebody else entirely: a dark-skinned woman. I blinked, thinking it was just a perceptual illusion, a trick of the light. As quickly as the image appeared, it disappeared, leaving me wondering if I had just imagined it.

"Stop questioning it!" came a voice into my mind, making me jump. I don't usually hear voices. As I looked in the mirror again, the face returned, smiling. I sat blinking, rubbing my eyes, and then blinking some more. The image became clearer until I could no longer distinguish the presence of a mirror. It was as if I were sitting across from this woman. She had short, dreadlocked hair with just a touch of gray in it. She wore billowy, colorful clothing and had a glow about her. She was beautiful.

"Hello," she said. "I'm Matrina. I've been waiting for you. It's taken you quite a while to get here."

"Wha...?"

"You think *I* came to *you*?"

I hardly knew what to think.

"No, Wrenne. You've come to me. I knew you would. I've been expecting you."

I sat there, mouth hanging open, unable to form words. She didn't rush me. She just matched my breathing in what I think was an attempt to calm me. When I realized she wasn't going to disappear again, I asked, "Oh God, this is it, isn't it? I've finally fallen off my rocker. Or is this like *Alice in Wonderland* or something? Or am I dead?"

"No, you're not dead, child. You're more alive than you've ever been. I've been calling you for a long time, and now you're finally here. Now I can share a very special gift I've kept for you."

"What?"

"You'll see."

And with that, she was gone, and I was staring at myself again.

෨ ෬

By the next morning, I had pretty much convinced myself that I had eaten something bad or just imagined my encounter with Matahari or Marina or whatever she said her name was. Maybe I couldn't remember her name, but what she said and how she felt stuck with me the way a sweet dream lingers upon waking. And like a dream, it began to fade all too quickly. I was grateful it was a Saturday and debated giving myself the pleasure of sleeping late, as I had nothing to do until much later in the day. Instead, I opted for getting up, taking a nice, hot shower, and making my favorite breakfast: buckwheat pancakes with avocado and banana.

In the bathroom, I stared in the mirror for a long time, looking at my sleepy face and remembering the stranger's face I'd seen last night. Would she reappear? She didn't. So I went about brushing my teeth, looking in the mirror every so often just in case. The hot water of the shower felt so great that I couldn't help but make an *AH* sound.

"*AH!* The perfect sound to awaken. It's the sound of prayer, a heart sound."

Hearing that voice, I slipped and nearly pulled the shower curtain down. When I peeked out, there was Matrina sitting on the toilet seat.

"Oh, sorry," she said beaming up at me with big brown eyes. "You might want to get used to me dropping in like this. It's going to happen."

I turned off the water and grabbed my towel. "Christ! You scared the crap out of me! What are you doing in here? How did you even get in?"

"You'll find that I don't obey the laws of physics. I'm sorry I startled you. I've never figured out how to appear without freaking people out. I thought the introduction in the mirror last night would help."

"I, ah, think I need to sit down. I feel dizzy."

She got up off the toilet seat and offered it to me. "You'll be fine. Just breathe, child. Try a nice *ZOOM* sound." And with that, she began making the sound *ZOOM*. So I joined her. After just a few seconds, I started to feel present in my body again.

"Wow, that really works. Thanks."

"You're most welcome. *ZOOM* is a powerful grounder. It takes the energy of the lower plexi and thrusts it down into the earth."

I repeated the sound a few more times trying to understand what she was talking about. "I think I can feel that...what you just said." I nodded toward the door. "Um, I'm dripping all over the place. Would you mind?"

"Oh. Of course not. I'll be right outside."

ഓ ൙

Once I'd dried off and dressed...and quite frankly, recovered my wits...I pulled open the door half-expecting the house to be empty. But there Matrina stood, looking at the books on my shelf. She looked like a tribal priestess, glowing with a youth that was contradictory to her age.

"You can learn so much from a person's book collection. You don't have very many, but I really like the ones you have!"

"Thank you."

"Like this one, for example: *The Music of Life* by Hazrat Inayat Khan. That's a great one."

"I'm embarrassed to say it took me about five years to read. Not because it was a long book or hard to read or anything. I mean, I'm not stupid. It was just so...full."

"Oh, this is going to be fun. You already understand so much already."

"Excuse me?"

"The book took you so long to read because it was written by a master who understood what he was doing. There are volumes within each sentence."

"That's it exactly. Reading just a few sentences was all I could process at one time. Matrinka..."

"Matrina," she interrupted to correct me.

"Sorry. Matrina, what are you here to show me?"

She pulled *The Music of Life* off the shelf and held it up.

"But I already read the book...several times now."

"Not the book, silly. The title."

And that's how my lessons with the magical and profound being who called herself Matrina began.

Invitation

"I've been watching you for a long time, child."

"That's a little eerie."

"Come now. I know you're aware that you're never alone, but looked after by teams of beings interested in your well-being."

"You mean like angels?"

"Angels, guides—by any name, nothing is ever hidden to them. There's nothing to be embarrassed or ashamed about."

"I can think of plenty of things."

"The point is, I know you. I understand you. I *see* you. And I'm here to help you. I'm not here to teach what you can find elsewhere. There are other sources you can turn to if you want to learn about the fundamentals. Of course, you're not a beginner, so I won't treat you like one."

"Beginner at what? What exactly are we talking about here?"

"Toning, sound healing, and the mysticism of words."

"But I *don't* know very much about that. Maybe we *should* start at the beginning."

"You've spent lifetimes on this stuff, my dear. You are a master already. You just don't realize it yet because you've been using that mastery for self-sabotage instead of self-benefit. That's all about to change. I'm here to inspire you with a provocative perspective that will lead you to your own explorations. This is an invitation. Do you accept?"

Her invitation created a storm of thoughts in my mind. She wasn't a large woman...not at all...but she seemed to fill the entire room with her presence. I had to close my eyes to her expectant expression and imposing energy just to think straight. This woman suddenly and magically appears in my life, tells me things I barely comprehend, and then says she's there to help me master what I've already mastered. Who is she? What does she want from me? What does she expect of me? What if she isn't who she says she is? What if this is all some kind of trick or temptation? Am I actually going insane here or is something of spiritual significance actually happening to me...ME!

Seeing the confusion, doubt, and bewilderment in my face, Matrina said, "I can see you need some time to sort out your thoughts, but let me just say this isn't really a decision for the mind. You've got to ask your heart what it wants. I'll be back for your answer."

ᔏᔑ

I didn't sleep much that night. I didn't know how to feel what my heart wanted, and my mind continued to battle itself with logistics. I weighed the pros and cons of accepting Matrina's offer. I even prayed to the God I thought I'd stopped believing in. I was terrified to commit to something when I had no understanding of what I was getting myself into, yet I couldn't seem to let go of the idea. I felt like a bone in the teeth of a dog. Would I have to quit my job? Would she expect payment? Would I have to move to India or something?

That morning, still undecided and panicked, I finally flipped a coin. Heads, yes; tails, no. The coin fell right out of my hands, rolled across the hardwood floor, spun around a few times, and settled...tails up. My heart sank in that moment, and I knew it had spoken. My heart's answer was "Yes!"

"Fantastic!" Matrina appeared the instant I had my unwavering answer. She dove right into the first lesson. "Do you ever get the feeling that words don't quite cut it anymore?" she asked.

After I nodded, she continued. "We can no longer express with words our emotional states, our revelations, our transformations. Words fail. We are in the very beginning stages of what might take years or even decades of transition. The human race is developing a Universal Language. The practices that will assist humanity—and assist you—in reaching this higher communication will include all the things I'll share with you: vocal exploration, meditation, and energetic practices such as chi gong and yoga. Through these techniques, you are going to completely overhaul your nervous system and your energetic makeup to allow the emergence of this language within you."

To be honest, half the time she spoke, I had no clue what she was talking about. Yet some part of me did understand.

Matrina continued.

"Humanity must pull its faith out of the symbols we call words and begin to write new dictionaries. We must redefine words that hold a negative charge, liberate words that are misused, and reclaim those that have held us in throes. This is more important than ever, as words are being used to manipulate on such a massive scale."

"Boy, that's for sure. Everything seems so upside-down these days. I can't bear to watch the news anymore because I no longer believe any of it. I feel powerless to change anything. Are you saying there's something I can do?"

"Change starts with each individual. We must begin to exercise new ways of being, creating, and dreaming with words. We must pull the sword of our impeccability from the stone of tradition and reclaim our throne as King of our castle. This is the true meaning of the return of the King. It isn't one person, some savior out there, but you and me—all of us."

"Sounds like the Arthurian legend."

"The mythology doesn't really matter. It's all the same story. Humanity must begin to use vitalized breath in very focused ways—for example, through toning and glossolalia."

"Vita-what? Through what-ails-ya?"

She ignored my confusion. I noticed she had this annoying habit of not answering my questions sometimes, but I came to understand that she simply didn't want to entertain my need to know. "We must free our right brains and the entire mechanism, material and immaterial, of the throat center. We must give reverence to Sacred Sound and practice in community with one another."

"You've lost me."

"Only your mind thinks that—the part of you that wants to understand everything I say by categorizing it and packaging it up according to your current perspective. But I say to you true, my message is getting through. Just take a moment. Don't think. Let go. Then I'll continue."

That was a bit of a challenge given the intensity of my shock over everything—the mirror, a woman suddenly appearing in my bathroom, and all the talk about things I've never heard of. Still, I did my best to follow her advice. I spent a few moments breathing deeply and then nodded.

"To affect change, you must begin to show up vocally in unusual circumstances and places, boldly breaking convention and social norms. You must help humanity free itself from its vocal paralysis, restoring Free Will and Free Speech. Engage others with an uninhibited spirit and wake yourselves from sleep. Spread out in all directions, appear in sudden moments, and brandish the wand of the fifth chakra upon the slumbers of the unconscious."

"Wow, this is all very…woo woo." I lived in a city among the flakier of flakes, but this was taking the cake.

Matrina ignored this too and continued.

"It's time to educate one another so we begin to recognize the tool that lies dormant in song. Learn the subtleties of vibration and the impact our voices have on ourselves—our very DNA!— on each other, and on our world. Open your eyes to see. Sound penetrates into many dimensional realms.

"Use sound as you walk through your day, reinforcing love here and dismantling fear and illusion there. Use sound to clean up our messes, our buildings, our planet, the water, the very air, and our relationships. It can be done. Once we recognize that sound can pollute, we can take measures to counteract the damage caused from decades of our ignorance.

"It's time to use sound to communicate with physical objects, the astral realms, our intuition, and our mental bodies. We must use sound to communicate with our very bodies and to help us alter our nervous systems for the coming changes. We must use sound to communicate with the No Sound, the Source of all that is."

I'm pretty sure I was drooling by this point, my mouth flopped open, my eyes wide, one eyebrow raised in incredulity.

"I'm speaking a Universal Language that is merely clothed in English. You are going to learn to do the same. Your speech must be as free from the contamination of mental constructs as possible. It has to be—you have to be—completely free of fear."

"I'm feeling a bit overwhelmed here. I mean...man, I don't know what I mean. This sounds so exciting, but so confusing too. It almost sounds like *you're* speaking another language."

"There is nothing you need to do except listen. The energy stored within each word I speak will do the rest. It will awaken you if you allow it. Are you ready?"

I merely nodded.

"This is a call, an invitation, to the initiation of reclaiming your Voice. Not the little voice with which we speak or sing daily. This is the Voice with a capital *V*, the voice of your creation, the Voice of Life."

Matrina made a *V* with her fingers, like a peace sign and placed them at her throat. As she did so, I noticed a light emanating from her hyoid bone, the area at the base of her throat where there really is a little *V*. It startled me. I wondered if she knew she was glowing. A look came over her, full of ferocity yet filled with love.

"For a very long time, the Voice has been patiently waiting for you to bring it into full consciousness. This is a call to awaken the lion that sleeps. You've been wielding your words like feathers for so long, when all along they were more like swords, piercing your mind with their poisoned tips, striking out at yourself and those you love and those who are different from you. For so long, you've accepted your universe and all of the concepts in it without question, unknowingly using words to fortify your dark and lonely castle when you could have used them to create a beautiful, inviting garden. For so long now, something else has held the power of the word and used it against you and the people you love. No more.

"In accepting this invitation, you are not promising anything to me or anyone else. You are making a promise to yourself with full consciousness. You are making a promise to become aware of the units we call words and to reclaim the power in every symbol you speak. You are promising to end gossip in every dimension, speaking only of what you truly know and only of those present to hear. You are promising especially to clean up the gossip you spread about yourself, whether in your own mind or out loud. No more disempowering yourself or anyone else ever again. You are promising to use your words to inspire and create joy, peace, and abundance with no conditions.

"I don't know what will happen when you say 'Yes.' It's your path and yours alone. I do know, however, that it will be a wonderful and mysterious journey along which you will encounter many challenges and receive many rewards. It can be the single most powerful and loving act of self love you could ever grant yourself."

I felt tears come to my eyes.

"The meaning of life is the meaning you give it," she continued. "That sounds so simple to understand, but this is one truth that resounds in every reflection of your life. You are the creator. If you can surrender your need to understand this or to deny it, you can begin to understand the importance of reclaiming your Voice."

I felt something happening for sure. My heart was racing. It felt like every cell in my entire body was bouncing with wild anticipation to be reunited with this truth, this remembering.

"The word is a powerful tool, powerful beyond human understanding. Every word that takes form in our minds or comes out of our mouths is a brick in the scaffold of our reality. If we were in our right minds, we'd be experiencing a world of immeasurable respect, justice, and love. If. But we are not sane. In fact, as a species, we've been very ill. Our gift of words has been hijacked by something that would gladly see us destroy ourselves rather than relinquish its control. In the *Toltec* mythology, which predates the Aztec, this something is likened to a parasite or predator. Others may call it the ego, but really, that just confuses people and makes the ego the enemy.

"It's time to become more conscious of how we use our voices — whether we write, speak, or simply think. More importantly, we must do this in ways unrelated to the trappings of our language so we can sidestep the hijacker and express ourselves from the place of our integrity. Once we strengthen that integrity, we are then free to return to language with greater wisdom, greater mindfulness, and greater compassion for ourselves and others. It's not that we worship the power of the word as a god in itself, but rather we begin to treat it with the utmost respect and humility. The word is one of the most powerful tools that we as creative beings can wield."

Matrina took a breath, cocked her head, and then smiled at me. I smiled back wondering if I was supposed to say something, but frankly, my mind had gone blank.

"So what is your intent?" she asked.

"I have good intentions, I think."

"Not intention. I have no interest in an intention that's simply one of many possibilities. I'm interested in intent, child — the one possibility that manifests — the meaning you give your life. What are you creating with your word choice, your rhythm, your tone, your volume, your articulation, and your timbre?"

"I...I don't know."

"It is time to find out. This is *my* intent—to bring you back to the Voice with a capital *V*, to lead you to a glorious and shining light in this and every moment on the wave of a breath, a sound, and silence."

Was this for real? My judging mind kept thinking that this woman was a complete loon. I was embarrassed by some of the sappy things she was saying. And yet...

"I don't know what to say. I'm excited and scared and bewildered! This is amazing!"

"Say yes!"

"Yes!"

The 1st Gate: Tongue in Cheek

I'd known Matrina for only a week and was still working hard to resolve my mixed feelings. I just couldn't figure her out. She not only seemed to know what I was thinking, she already seemed to know so much about me and my past. It was unsettling. Who...*what* was this woman?

She was understanding of my doubts. In fact, she said we both just needed a little time to get to know and trust her new human form...not exactly a comforting thought, but her big brown eyes, like cups of hot cocoa, made up for it. They held a heat that could sweeten and warm me right up no matter what mental confusion I was entertaining. I melted like a marshmallow in those eyes.

I asked her something that had been on my mind.

"Matrina, you said my work with you was going to help me to sing better."

"Absolutely."

"So basically you're just going to give me voice lessons? Because, you know, I've had voice lessons before."

"Child, you haven't had voice lessons like this, and it's a good thing you haven't had too many of any other kind either. You won't have as much to unlearn."

Matrina sat me down in front of my mirror. It was a little bizarre seeing her in the mirror with me. It was like she had stepped through the glass.

"Open your mouth," she urged. "I want you to look inside."

I opened my mouth.

"Wider. It's almost like you're holding on the edge of a yawn. That's better. Now, what do you see?"

I spoke like I do in the dentist's chair..."Eh seh muh ung, ed ih-s you"...until I realized I could close my mouth to speak normally. "I see my tongue, red tissue, the uvula, my teeth, the opening at the back..."

"Good. Look again. Notice what your tongue is doing. Notice the different placements it can take. Did you know it's one of the strongest muscles in the body?"

My eyes popped open in surprise. "O, eh I en't." (No, I didn't.)

"Isn't it interesting that the tongue is considered a very important organ for diagnosis in Chinese Medicine? It sits in the mouth, a large opening of the body that leads into and past the voice box, down the esophagus, and through many important organs, out the other end. The tongue is like a gatekeeper, monitoring everything that passes into the body through the mouth. It protects our most vulnerable innards from outside influences. The food we ingest is both tasted and digested with the help of the tongue. And of course, the tongue is necessary to form all the sounds of our language."

"I've never really given much thought to my tongue before."

"The tongue may also serve the role of a trap door, determining what *leaves* the body as well. The tongue may in effect stop anything that arises within us as we attempt to swallow our feelings, for example, or keep our thoughts to ourselves. Shall we continue?"

"Uh-huh." I was starting to get drowsy, like I was being hypnotized.

"Isn't it also interesting that in our collective consciousness, we hold so much trauma around the throat?"

When she said that, she struck me lightly but briskly on the back. With the surprise, time and space collapsed. The room disappeared around me, and nothing remained to help me orient myself. I was thrust down a tunnel, spinning and flailing. I emerged as a woman in an old German village, wearing a torturous device on my head that painfully pulled my tongue out of my mouth and made it impossible for me to speak. I saw myself as a spy, and they were cutting my tongue right out of my mouth. I then saw life after life of gruesome torture and punishment for speaking, praying, expressing, preaching, and practicing various arts that had been deemed heretical, evil, dangerous, or just oppositional. And it didn't stop with tongue trauma. I saw others experience throat cuttings, hangings, burnings, dunkings, and beheadings. Over many lifetimes, I was both the persecuted and the persecutor.

I was sure I was drowning now as I coughed, fighting to emerge through what seemed like the frozen surface of water, cold and unforgiving. When light broke through my eyes, I again found myself in my living room, staring at the mirror, as an unbelievably guttural sound rose up from my root chakra...an energy center of my body...and escaped through my mouth, curdling the very air around me. I collapsed in tears, pain emanating from my throat. I felt a pulsing of energy as if there were some creature inside my tissues about to break loose.

Matrina didn't move, but I felt her strong and reassuring presence at my side. After several minutes of this release, she handed me a tissue.

"Very good," she said, placing a hand tenderly on my head. "When you surrender, you don't resign. This is different. Surrender is a sweetness that comes from loving what is and letting go. That's all we'll do for today."

Surrender-schmender! What had I gotten myself into? So far, this was not my idea of fun.

౫౦ Q3

I didn't see Matrina again for a good week, but I felt so different. I felt like my entire throat was more...expanded. I can't describe it better than that. I just felt more whole, more myself. When Matrina did show up, she appeared as a light, like the bubble Glenda the Good Witch used in the *Wizard of Oz*. It was familiar and comforting.

"I thought you might like that," she said, proud of herself. "Didn't want to startle you again. So how are you doing?"

"I feel really good. I can't believe it! I'm not entirely sure what happened in our last session together, but the effect was really amazing."

"Ready for more?"

"I don't know if I'm ready for more past lives or whatever, but I'm ready to feel more of what I'm feeling now if that's possible."

"There's no need to dwell in the past—once you've fully experienced it. So, what have you noticed since last time?"

"Well, my throat feels more open somehow. Now that I think about it, words seem to flow out more easily. Everything is more relaxed."

"Notice how you're built. The neck is literally a bottleneck. We have these wide heads that sit on this little neck, and then we spread out into these wide bodies. Energy has to flow both in and down and up and out. When the throat is blocked, it can't do any of that."

I sat in front of the mirror again, and Matrina coached me to open my mouth and gaze inside. She mentioned how important it was to breathe a very even, rhythmic breath. After several minutes, I went into a very deep trance state.

"Today, I just want you to follow the channel of your throat, the pipe from your gut to your mouth out and from your mouth to your gut in. That's it. This is an invitation, a chance for you to reprogram this channel. To do that, we need to wipe your existing program. That program is comprised of every unexpressed emotion, opinion, and truth you've ever held back. It's also comprised of every belief and opinion from the outside that you ate and integrated, many of which are only in your way. All that blocked stuff locks you down to this day."

Sitting at my side, Matrina pointed two fingers at my throat and made a counterclockwise circular motion. Everything around me went soft and mushy, pulsing in and out.

"Now just breathe in and out of your mouth. Look into the mirror. Gaze right past your tongue and down your throat. That's it. Breathe easy. Let your gaze become soft. Allow whatever is there to reveal itself to you. Now use your imagination to move down that pipe, throat to gut. Feel the channel."

As I traveled down my throat, I started to feel energy rising up, like I was awakening spirits from their dormant slumber. So many words I'd choked back in fear of rejection or hurting someone I loved. So many conversations swallowed in fear of being judged or ostracized. Wave after wave of phrases and incomplete expressions came wafting past me like fog, rising up and out. I began whimpering and then screaming, "No! Stop it!" and "You're hurting me!" and "Liar!" Each outburst was unrelated to the one before it and impossible to relate to *anything* really. They moved so quickly, I couldn't pinpoint what precipitated the outbursts. I was choking, making animal-like noises, and then all of a sudden laughing.

Through each experience, Matrina was right there with me, coaching me like a midwife. "It's all good," she said. "Let it out. Don't let the mind get on it and censor any of it." She explained that I was releasing energy I'd been holding onto since childhood.

After a final fit of laughter, everything in me relaxed. I was sweating and exhausted, flat on my back. Matrina covered me with a blanket and began humming. It was beautiful, nurturing...and something else. I felt things inside me being reorganized, directed by the sound of her voice.

"That, child, was the first gate. Don't worry. It gets easier."

Too exhausted to reply, I simply hoped that would prove true.

2nd Gate: Breathe Deeply

Despite the challenges (to put it lightly) I faced when working with Matrina, I began to look forward to her visits. There was something about this woman, a grace or deep calm that emanated from her, influencing my own state of mind in such positive ways. After another week of working with the tongue and throat, my lessons with her thankfully began to subtly alter course.

"We have one more thing to do," Matrina told me, "before we move on to the next gate. We'll begin with a breathing exercise and then move right into a throat activation."

"Activation?"

"Call it the installation of the new program. It will prepare your throat for the work ahead. It will help accelerate your process."

"Will it hurt?"

"No, of course not, child. Now sit up straight."

I put my feet on the floor with my back against a chair.

"Inhale one, deep breath, and then release it deliberately and evenly."

My nerves quelled with the breath.

"Prepare to give to yourself. Gently tip your chin toward the ceiling as far up as is comfortable. Hold your head in this position, keeping your neck long and stretched. Now inhale and hold your breath at the top. Now arms out in front of you. That's it. Palms stretched up toward the ceiling."

It was a little awkward, but I could feel a pressure building at the front of my neck.

"With your breath held, see if you can tense and release your stomach muscles, pumping your stomach in and out. That's it. Good. Now exhale. With the breath held out, begin to pump your stomach in and out again."

We did this for only a minute or so, but it was the longest minute of my life.

"Now gently drop your head back down, bringing your chin down to rest on your chest, stretching the back of the neck."

It felt great to release the tension of holding my head back. The stretch forward was a relief, but I could also feel how this difficult exercise had stimulated my throat.

"With your head down, clasp your hands together behind you and raise your arms up off your back. Now breathe in and begin to pump your stomach in and out once more. Exhale. Good. Now pump your stomach with the breath held out. Good."

I could feel something happening within my throat...a heat was building; a pulsing sensation was growing.

"Gently bring your head back to center and turn your head slowly to the right to look behind you. Good. Now slowly to the left. Prepare to receive. Now with your head center again, relax and release any tension."

I felt even more energy pulsing at my throat.

"Bring your attention to the area of the throat where that little *V* is at the base of your neck, right at the hyoid bone. Within that chalice, see a liquid light glowing and radiating, upward and outward like a pulsar. As you focus on this light, it becomes warm and golden. It begins to drip like honey—up, down, and in all directions—coating and soaking into every tissue, bone, and cell—of your throat, neck, larynx, vocal folds, tongue, thyroid, and parathyroid. Everything relaxes. The deepest of holdings, the most rooted obstructions, the most secret longings, and the most insistent fears are being penetrated by this light."

It was wild. My muscles were twitching.

"That's it. Let go of past trauma, betrayal, heartache, and despair. It's now transmuted effortlessly in this golden light. Energy is moving and pulsing. It's free and alive. The wheel at your throat is spinning and opening like a colorful pinwheel riding the breeze—every color of the spectrum, there in your very own voice."

In my mind's eye, I could actually see this explosion of psychedelic color.

"When you're in flow with life, your voice is fluid and ever-transforming, like the images you see when you turn the dial of a kaleidoscope. But what tends to happen to you? You fixate on an idea of who you are, and suddenly all that you could be becomes stuck on one fixed image. 'I am like this. I am like that. I can't do this. I don't do that.' Yet each of us has so much untapped potential—so many gradients of colorful expressions.

"So give yourself permission to explore all your colors and let them show! Imagine the entire channel of your throat revealing itself as a rainbow crystal palace, the very walls of your throat clear and transparent. As each color of the rainbow is refracted through the prism of your vocal mechanism, a glorious, victorious white light breaks through, emanating outward. Your entire body smiles with joy and relief! Allow yourself to express a sound from that place: a tiny sigh, a little moan, whatever feels right."

I laughed. I felt so light, so happy.

"Or even a bright laugh! From this place—staying very deep, very connected—repeat with me each letter of the alphabet: *A*, *B*, *C*—Come on! You know them."

I felt a little silly repeating my *ABCs* like a schoolgirl, but I followed her lead.

When we finished, Matrina stood and placed her hands at her throat. "You see? This very bottleneck that can make voice work so difficult is also what makes this work so powerful. The throat is a condenser of energy. It works like a laser when it's clean and clear. It can influence timelines and change history." She looked at me and smiled. "You've done good work today."

∞ ⊗

After my "activation," I started to have some pretty strange dreams. In one, I was standing knee deep in the middle of a river. As I stood there, letters and words began to rain down from the sky over my body, and when I looked down, I realized I wasn't standing in water, but in a river of concepts. They were all being washed away in the current. It gave me a sense of newness and freedom. I felt pure and clean.

Matrina told me the next gate would work on my breathing. Over the next few weeks, I was astounded to discover how often I held my breath, how it would change in different circumstances, and how using it consciously could change the way my nervous system responded to stimuli. By breathing deeply before a telephone call I didn't want to make, for example, I was much less anxious and able to keep myself centered despite the challenging conversation.

I also learned to curb and eventually eliminate the panic attacks I'd sometimes get in the middle of the night. They came out of the blue and for no apparent reason, but by simply breathing deeply, I was able to communicate to my brain and body that I wasn't in any danger.

"Be grateful for the force of creation the breath provides. Without the breath, there would be no singing, no vocal expression, no life!"

"I *am* grateful for my breathing."

"Hmm, but you forget to enjoy it!" Matrina took a deep, relaxed breath with a smile. "Do you know how powerful words can be? Did you know they can impact a person's state of mind like nothing else?"

"I can think of plenty of times when I got insanely angry or terribly hurt after hearing someone say a certain string of words."

"So much for sticks and stones! While we all recognize the power of words, we don't realize that it's the force behind our words that holds a much greater power. We might mistakenly think this power is simply the breath, which we can control. But really, what we know as 'breathing' is not the actual breath. Sure, we can feel ourselves breathing air in and out, but the current of the breath is beyond perception. This mystery, this current, is the soul. It runs much deeper than what we think of as 'breathing.' It's our connection to God. Hence the word *inspiration*."

"Right. *Inspire* comes from the Latin *in* and *spiritus*. In spirit."

"Try this little experiment. Feel the breath as it flows through your nose, in and out. Bring your attention there and just notice how it feels, how far it reaches."

I closed my eyes and breathed in and out of my nose. The sensation was very close to home, so to speak; I could feel a gentle rush of air passing ever so slightly beyond the field of my physical body.

"Now feel the breath as it flows through your mouth, like when you're blowing out a candle."

I tried it. This breath had more direction. I could see the air impacting the world around me as it left my body. The leaf of a plant on the table in front of me trembled as my breath passed.

"Finally, there's the breath that carries sound, such as a whistle or a tone. It's charged with a mysterious quality, isn't it? It penetrates and reaches out, even more so than a touch can, although a touch might feel more solid."

"That makes sense to me. I mean, even walls don't stop sound waves. My voice could conceivably go on and on." I made a tone and could feel a strong directional quality within the breath, like a laser.

Matrina looked at me like she wanted to say something about that, then changed her mind. "The practice of vocal toning is vitalized breath. Obviously, you cannot tone unless you have the breath to do it, and you cannot tone well without the ability to control your breath. Your control is proportionate to the duration, power, and quality of your tones. If you want a stronger voice, toning is a great practice for improving its quality. Toning will also help you to find your equilibrium and power with breathing."

"That sounds great. Am I going to learn vocal toning?"

"Eventually. But first, we have several other gates to walk through. For starters, I'm going to show you several breathing exercises you can practice throughout the week ahead. With each of them, be as gentle and as present as you can be. Air is the element that makes sounding possible. Breathing isn't just about sucking in air and pushing it out again. There's more to it than that. The diaphragm creates a vacuum and then restores equilibrium, but what's directing the diaphragm? What's in charge of the involuntary process of breathing?"

"Um...I don't know."

"That's because it's a mystery. So naturally, it's important to do exercises that help us explore this mystery and build breath control. The first requires one of these." She produced a plastic straw and handed it to me.

"A straw?" I tore away the paper wrapping.

"Simply breathe through your mouth in and out of the straw. The straw is a contained space, so you have to control your breath. It's like lifting weights to build muscle. You're building breath control."

I did as she instructed.

"Good. Breathe all the way down into your abdomen while keeping your shoulders down and relaxed. You may feel a little anxious; that's okay. You can stop and breathe normally at any time."

I did feel a little panicky, as if I wasn't getting enough oxygen. And then I yawned.

"Yep, good. You'll probably find yourself wanting to yawn a lot at first." She indicated for me to put the straw aside. "Okay, the second exercise is called The Snake. Place your top and bottom teeth together, tongue relaxed. Now breathe in through your nose and hiss when you exhale."

I hissed and quickly ran out of air.

"Not quite so forcefully. See if you can keep the exhalation gentle and even-keeled without bursting out or rushing. Sssssuper! Keep the breath very even as you breathe in through your nose. Now exhale through the teeth in a measured hiss."

We practiced that breath for a minute or so, at which point I couldn't stifle another yawn.

"Getting tired?"

I nodded.

"Let's do one more." Matrina walked to the table where my goldfish George was happily doing nothing. She called me over. "His name is George, right? Notice how his mouth opens and closes in the water. The water goes in, the water goes out. There's no effort other than opening and closing his mouth. That's the general idea here. Open your mouth as if you had no jaw muscles to keep it closed. Let it drop relaxed. Relax your tongue away from the back of the throat without pushing down. Now just inhale and exhale out of your mouth without effort. Be George. Only instead of water, you're experiencing the flow of air in and out."

I bent over and looked at George, who looked back at me. Together, we practiced breathing for a minute or so. He seemed to enjoy the camaraderie.

"Wow, I like that one. It's so relaxing."

"I want you to keep working with these exercises during the week ahead. Notice if your breathing changes in any way as a result. Also notice any reactions that may come up." Matrina turned to the fish tank. "Thanks for your help, George."

I could swear he winked.

ℬℭ

I was sitting outside drinking in the sun's light, enjoying one of the warmest of Spring days. I took a deep breath and enjoyed its path through my lungs, all earth- fragrant and crisp. All week,

I'd been noticing times when I wasn't breathing…like when I was driving in my car or reading something irritating online. Matrina's exercises were really increasing my awareness.

"How's the breathing?"

"Oh. Hi, Matrina. It's good. I practiced all three techniques you showed me. They definitely got a lot easier over time. I don't get as anxious."

"That's very good. I think you're ready for more. When you received that voice transmission a few weeks ago, I had you do a breathing exercise with the pumping movement, remember?"

I nodded.

"It's called Breath of Fire. It's an ancient yogic practice. Let's start there. To get a feel for it, begin to pant lightly through the mouth like a dog. Keep your breath even when you inhale and exhale. You should feel the quick pulses of your diaphragm as the air moves in and out."

I did as she requested, feeling my tongue dry out.

"Now, instead of doing that through an open mouth, close your mouth and breathe through your nose." Matrina demonstrated. "You can do it slowly or if you're comfortable, more rapidly. Relax. Be easy. Let it happen. With each exhalation, bring your belly button in as if you were trying to touch your spine with it."

After a couple of minutes, Matrina stopped and said, "Take in a nice, big cleansing breath and hold it for a moment. Good. Now let it go and breathe normally. Give yourself a moment to just be."

After a few breaths, I said, "That's a workout!"

"Yes, it is. An aerobic one, very beneficial. Sun Breathing is your next exercise. Here, the idea is to use your breath to pull in the energy of the sun." She looked up at the bright yellow ball over our heads. "As you inhale its light, place your hands on various parts of your body to apply a gentle pressure that impacts and responds to your breath. Begin by placing your hands on your chest, applying a gentle pressure."

I did so. It was getting easier to follow her instructions.

"Now breathe in, maintaining that pressure, and feel the sunlight and air pushing the lungs outward against the pressure. See if you can continually expand the breath on each inhale, filling yourself with more and more light."

I soon discovered this breath was aptly named. I felt myself becoming as bright as the sun, from the inside out.

"Now put your hands around your waist, thumbs toward the back. Again, apply a gentle pressure around the barrel of your ribcage. Breathe in the sun."

I could feel my rib cage expand out against the pressure from my hands. When I exhaled, I could feel my rib cage collapse. I had done exercises like this before in other voice lessons, but breathing in the warmth from the sunlight added a whole new dimension.

As if reading my thoughts, Matrina said, "All light holds information. The sun has a beautiful message to share with each of us. Good. Again, direct the inhalation toward expanding your rib cage. Exhale. Relax. You can apply this pressure when breathing to just about anywhere on your body to help direct your healing intent to soreness or pain and to help you increase your oxygen intake. The light provides information to the body to help you heal and open in preparation for growth—just like it does for plants."

I tried placing my hands over my kidneys, my solar plexus, and even my knees.

"Instead of applying pressure, you can also lightly tap your body using a cupped palm like this." She demonstrated. "In this variation, tap first, pause, then breathe in and out. Don't try to tap and breathe at the same time. You can tap your upper chest, your solar plexus, the sacral area, your lower back, or your shoulders."

"Can we break now?" I was beginning to feel quite tired.

"Yes, I'm sorry. This is intensive."

"I'm exhausted, but I also feel better…more relaxed. There's a buzz growing in my veins. I actually feel brighter."

"Perfect! Experiment with these techniques until I return. We'll see how it goes, and maybe I'll show you some more. I'll leave you to it."

Thankfully, Matrina had been right. The work *was* getting easier. The initial histrionic episodes that seemed beyond my comprehension ceased. They were replaced with feelings of being fully grounded in myself and much more relaxed in my own skin.

PART II

NOTHING BUT WORDS

The fire of words alights my soul in a blaze
Each syllable, each consonant and vowel alive
rising and falling like a seesaw
Falling from my mind like the juices of ripe fruit
I love to play within the alphabet
I love to make music with letters
I love to express what could only come from this one
These hot specks burn me to the core of me
Melt me down into radioactive particles
Spin me on the merry go round of words
words, words are a playground we have forgotten

The 3rd Gate: Letters to the Editor

I've been fascinated with letters and words for a long time. So when Matrina began delving into this topic with me, I was ripe with anticipation, even if I didn't understand its connection to my voice yet. In fact, one of my earliest memories was of sitting with a huge book of nursery rhymes on my lap, fingering the satiny pages, pretending to be reading while the illustrations came alive in my imagination.

"Did you know that *abracadabra* comes from the Aramaic *abraq ad habra*, which literally translates to 'I will create as I speak'?"

"Really? I did not know that. Cool."

"What's more amazing is how we habitually take the power of our voice for granted. When we bring our awareness to our voice and learn to express it in new ways—with impeccability—we rediscover our true message. *Your* voice is the key to unlocking the power and magnificence of your message. This work isn't about singing on key, finding the right words, leaving out 'ums' and 'uhs' and articulating clearly. This is about allowing and accepting your Magical Self. Let's talk about how words create you."

"Words create me? Isn't it the other way around? I create with words."

"Yes, that's also true, but it's not as important at the moment."

So began Matrina's lessons on letters and words: the 3rd Gate.

"All of Life—that mysterious, awesome, and impossible-to-know force—is repeatedly minimalized when we attempt to distill something immeasurable into the funny, clunky, unfulfilling little channels called words. Don't get me wrong; words are wonderful. I love them. I use them every day, and they serve a wonderful purpose—or at least they *can*."

"I understand. I often feel words fall short, like I'm always trying to express the inexpressible."

"Touché! While words allow us to share our thoughts, ideas, and feelings with others—never mind whether or not they even get it—to paint colorful pictures of what is and what may be, they can also plant ferocious little seeds of hatred, fear, and other poisons—especially when we fail to question what they mean or insist they mean only what we think they mean."

"At the risk of sounding impertinent, what do *you* mean?"

"Take *God*, for example. The word itself is completely empty. It's composed of three letters or individual sounds that when put together make one sound we recognize as the word. It's the sound that carries a powerful energy of the concept *God*. For one person, that word may mean very little. For another, it may mean one thing and one thing only. While for a third, it may mean something expansive and inclusive of many other concepts. The danger isn't in the word or sound so much as in our interpretation of it. People kill and die over that word."

"I'm with you. I actually had quite an experience with that right before I met you," I said referring back to my earlier insights about God. "It's a touchy subject for almost everyone. Please go on."

"Words were originally intended to be tools for us to master. But at some point in our evolution, everything got turned upside-down and words became *our* masters. Rather than defining these symbols for ourselves, we inherited the definitions put forth by our ancestors. What's even worse, these symbols became corrupted through misuse, manipulation, and out-and-out lies. A child being beaten by a parent heard 'I love you.' The politician whose actions repeatedly ignored the unconstitutional nature of new laws pledged 'justice for all.' People more concerned with their own rights than anyone else's gave lip service to 'equal rights.' In this age, our lack of consciousness around words is so great that when we are fed an endless diet of lies, we eat them without complaint. When we reawaken to the power of words, we'll awaken to our responsibilities as creators."

"I'm hungry," I said getting up and walking to the refrigerator. I realized I hadn't eaten in hours. "Can I get you something?"

"No, thank you. Sleepwalking through the dreamscape of words transcends verbal communication. For example, consider the way mainstream America buys items it calls *food* in the grocery store. Most of it is nothing more than highly processed, likely tainted, devoid-of-any-nutrient-value, artery- and liver-clogging, DNA-mutating, diabetes-inducing garbage."

"I guess I'm not as hungry as I thought," I said, closing the fridge and returning to the couch.

"As long as an authority figure says it's good for us—which is what we want to hear—that seems to be enough for most people. So we buy packaged products of refined, processed, and genetically modified materials. We ingest them and then ignore our bodies' responses. Or we take a pill to counteract the body's intelligence so we can go on poisoning ourselves. This contradiction between words and actions—or words and truth—has created a crisis of faith in the power of the word, which in turn has left many of us numb. Just as many food companies and grocery stores claim what they are selling is actually food, the media— TV, books, movies, and music—are also feeding us ideas."

"This is food?" I asked, lifting a book from the coffee table in front of us.

"Yes, but we'll get deeper into that at another time. These symbols—words—are programming us and our faith."

"Faith? You mean our belief in God?"

"When I say *faith*, I don't mean faith in religion. I mean the faith in our power as human beings to create this dream, this reality, our world, and our lives."

"So if our attention is constantly being diverted by symbols we didn't choose, what's the truth?"

"Great question! Reflect upon what's been happening since 9-11. We the public were told what to believe by a force we trusted.

We were told our safety was at risk and what had to be done."

"Sounds like you question it. That's rather un-American of you, Matrina."

"I do question it, and that's the point. You asked, 'What's the truth?' The only way to answer that unanswerable question is to keep asking it—over and over. We were led into a war based on a lie that has since led to the systematic collapse of our economy and the free market. We forfeited our power of discernment and ignored our intuition. In contrast, look at the reaction Norway took to a terrorist attack there."

"What did they do?"

"It's what they didn't do. They didn't rush into action. They took time to mourn. Then they decided that they wouldn't respond with fear. They chose instead to affirm their nation as one of peace."

I was feeling a little hot under the collar. "You mean, in America, we just ate up the fear? We didn't question what we were told or the approach our leaders took?"

"No, we didn't. The use of the symbols *crisis* and *terror* was enough to throw us into panic. We never really bothered to question if the crisis was real or even what those symbols might mean coming from different lips—let alone our own. We didn't even consider our options. We simply reacted, putting policies into place that are now entrenching themselves in our society. Myths are entrenching themselves in our history."

"Hey, I happen to like America. I'm a patriot."

"Do you like what is happening to it?"

She had me there.

"I'm not saying there is anything wrong with America—or any other country for that matter. I'm just using it as an example to help you see something very important—how misconceptions and lies can lead us down the wrong path. Ignorance is not bliss."

"But it sounds like you're saying we were wrong to defend

ourselves."

"That's irrelevant to my point. I'm saying once we knew we were deceived, nothing changed and no one in charge paid a price." She paused before going on. "Everything that's happening in the political and commercial landscapes of America is merely bringing into light what has been buried beneath generations of fear. We're running a very outdated program. If we contrast the American reaction to 9-11 with the actions taken after the bombing in Norway, another way is revealed. We have a choice to recommit ourselves to peace rather than revenge. We have a choice to commit ourselves to truth. To do that, we have to reclaim our power over the word."

"Are you saying words got us into this mess?"

"Yes, and I and my sisters are partly to blame. That's why I'm here now. And I pray you'll listen. The Bible says, 'In the beginning was the word, and the word was with God.' Whether you ascribe to the Bible as a book written by God or not, there is a very deep truth in that phrase. As our work unfolds, that truth will become evident."

She was partly to blame? She had sisters? The mystery that was my mysterious teacher deepened. But I tried to take in what I could and responded, "So, words are mere symbols representing things, but they aren't the things themselves? The word *teabag* is not a teabag. I get that. Seems like the danger then is in thinking otherwise…in believing in the word as the truth."

"Precisely. At one time, we were free of all these symbols. We experienced the truth of them instead. As babies, for example, we couldn't communicate or understand *rattle*. We relied on our feeling and experiential encounter with *rattle*. As we grew, we were trained with symbols and soon came to both understand them and use them. We could name the thing: rattle. But what did we really understand?"

"Not much beyond what we were taught to understand, I guess. It could just as easily have been called a *teabag*." I was beginning to realize that I could call anything whatever I wanted. If I could get people to agree with me, I'd have power over their perceptions. Similarly, when I entered into an agreement with others, they held power over me.

"Our knowledge is limited both by the limits of our teachers and by the natural inability for a word to represent something real. In that respect, words become a veil between our experience of the real and our imaginings of the real, complete with multi-layered projections. We lose sight of the difference. For example, if someone describes the color *purple* to a person who'd never seen it before, the description—any description—will fall short of an actual experience with the color. In addition, this person's new concept of purple is tinted—even tainted—by the first person's ability to describe it. What if the person describing it is prejudiced against purple or believes the color purple is evil? You see? But words can also become our liberation. When we question our concept of purple, we see it as if for the first time with no label. That's liberation! A dear friend used to say, 'Ugly is a unicorn.' I thought it was brilliant."

"I don't get it. Why is ugly a unicorn? Did she think unicorns were ugly?"

"Actually, it was a he. And no, nothing like that. We were talking about what it means to be ugly. Who decides something like that? Why was the word *ugly* ever even invented? *Ugly* is just a concept. It isn't real. No one, no thing is really ugly. It just is what it is. *Ugly* doesn't exist, like unicorns don't exist, at least not here. So 'ugly is a unicorn' means that *ugly* is a myth."

"That's weird, but I get it...I think."

"Have you ever read about when the Europeans crossed to the Americas for the first time? When the natives saw the ships, they just assumed they were clouds. They had no frame of reference for *ship*, so they couldn't see them. It was the medicine man of the village that began to recognize that something unknown was truly out there. When we begin to see what is, that too is liberation."

"So are you saying we only see something or someone as ugly because we know the word and understand the concept?"

"Basically. We communicate daily using hundreds of symbols. Do we really know what we're saying? Do we really know what anyone else is saying? We surely think we do. And of course, on some level, we do. When, for example, someone tells us not to put our hand on a hot burner, we understand the warning. But really, is what's hot to one person necessarily hot to another? And what if the person telling us not to put our hand on the burner was merely told by someone else not to put his hand on the burner by someone who was told not to put her hand on the burner—and now the burner is no longer hot?"

"That reminds me of an experiment I read about. A group of gorillas was placed in a cage, along with a bunch of bananas at the top of a ladder. When any gorilla started climbing the ladder, the others were sprayed with high-pressure hoses. When they pulled the gorilla off the ladder, the hoses stopped. The thing is, one by one, the gorillas were swapped out for a new set. Even though no hoses were turned on again, the new gorillas learned not to climb the ladder."

"Interesting. Makes you wonder what ladders you've learned not to climb, doesn't it? All of what we call knowledge is symbolic. Symbols gain their meaning from their distinction from other symbols, but we cannot articulate true reality. That's why so many masters have chosen to stay silent rather than teach. So we have a job to do at this, the 3rd Gate."

"What is that?"

"To become conscious of the words we speak and awaken to the power contained within them, to reclaim the meaning we inherited around symbols, and to create a new mental dictionary, if you will, that reflects a higher vision. Reclaiming our energy from symbols is neither quick nor easy, but it will definitely be rewarding. I have to go away for a while, though; I'm not sure for how long. I'd like you to just pay attention and stay open to whatever appears on this topic. We'll talk about it when I get back."

A small part of me felt abandoned. This seemed like a critical juncture in my training. Had I done something wrong? Matrina seemed to pick up on that.

"Where are you taking the symbol of my leaving?"

"Saw that, did you? I don't know. I feel like you're abandoning me. I know it's crazy, but the thought is there."

"So just notice the thought, but don't put any faith in it. This time apart is important. Trust me, child. I promise I'll be back soon. We'll pick up right where we left off."

∞ ∞

The first thing that happened during the month or so that Matrina was away was that I discovered the French philosopher Derrida. I didn't particularly understand everything he wrote, but he examined the idea that every word we speak is part of an existing framework. I got a feel for what he meant by practicing what he called *archi-écriture* or writing in air. By writing a word in thin air, I was creating an invisible structure right in front of me, one that held meaning and created an immediate connection to the word's *trace* or energy.

I interpreted it to mean that over time, we've infused words with so much meaning, examples, and emotions that now, just to write a word with your finger…let's say the word *love*…is enough to evoke the energies of anyone who had ever used the word previously. It really got me wondering what the heck words are. I mean, they are such small things that represent such complex ideas. How do they do that?

Derrida believed that authorship did not equal authority. While we give birth to text, it eventually takes on a life of its own. This very book you now hold is separate from its creator.

Everyone anywhere who reads it infuses it with new meaning. It is evolving even as you read it now.

As for each of us, we are like ghosts living a self of mental constructs. In a way, we are literally who we think we are, but *only* because we think so. I was really hoping Matrina would be able to shed some light on these ideas when she returned. I believed she could.

I also discovered the first book in the *Ringing Cedars* series. It's a book about a Russian mystic of sorts named Anastasia, who shared her wisdom with the man who later wrote the book. Within it was a passage that activated something in me. Anastasia related that all the books that have ever been written were composed of a finite number of letters in the alphabet. That means *War & Peace,* the Bible, *Little Women,* and even the latest issue of *Vogue* were all written with just 26 letters...at least the English-language versions. When I read that part of the story, something I couldn't describe...some dormant element of my DNA...lit up inside me. It was a piece that illuminated more of the puzzle of my life.

I had the idea then and there to meditate on each of the letters of the alphabet. It was going to be my personal project until Matrina returned. Every word in the English-speaking world, every single one, was made up using the same 26 letters! It felt like I had been given a glimpse beyond...or maybe through...the basic knowledge of the alphabet right to its mystical properties. Hadn't Matrina asked me to recite the alphabet when we had activated my throat early on in our work together? By reciting each letter with intent, maybe I could infuse it with magic so that every time I used that letter when I spoke, the energies with which I had programmed the letters would work upon those who heard them...including myself. This would elevate my prayers and strengthen my intent.

I began my new practice the following morning. I'd been doing some kundalini yoga Matrina taught me to help build up my nervous system, but this new meditation took an exciting precedence. I began. *A...B...C...* At first, nothing much happened. But I stuck with it, spending time with each letter, giving it my full attention. Then one morning, almost instantaneously, my heart opened up as I recited the letters. I felt in touch with something beautiful and beyond knowing. I wiped tears from my eyes, utterly amazed.

I continued my alphabet practice, saying each letter and only moving on when I felt a connection. I paid attention to any images or words that flashed in my mind. I consciously choose words as well...*D...death...divine...desire...* Then I began combining each consonant with each vowel...*Ba* as in Bach, *Ba* as in bay, and *Ba* as in bat. I did this categorically and with great concentration. Then I returned to simply reciting the alphabet in order. Until one day...

⁋Ȅ

"How are your explorations in Noetics going?"

"Matrina! I'm so happy to see you." I gave her a big hug. "What are Noetics?"

"The conscious and intentional use of language—or anything else for that matter."

"Oh! It's been amazing! I can't wait to tell you about it! I learned about this philosopher named Derrida, and I've been doing this wild meditation with the alphabet. I think I've discovered some magical key to the universe or something."

"Wonderful! The activation has taken effect. You are now reprogramming yourself. Did you know that the Kabbalists would recite the Hebrew alphabet as a practice? In fact, in the Kabbalist faith, it is believed that utterances of primal letters can give birth to golems or creatures made to do the bidding of their masters."

"No, I didn't know that." I felt simultaneously deflated that my idea wasn't original and elated that I'd tapped into something ancient.

"Other traditions too have very secretive mystery schools that practice magical works with the alphabet...regardless of the language."

"So, I really did stumble onto something. I didn't just make this up? How can I expand and strengthen this practice? Teach me! Teach me!"

"Relax, Grasshopper! That's why I'm here!" That was when Matrina finally told me who she really was: The Unknown Mother, a *Matrika*.

"I am Power given form. I am the Alphabet's Ruler and the Creator of Life's Song. I am Love personified just as I am the Thrust and Magnet of Timelessness."

Matrina was the embodiment of a goddess of universal consciousness. Matrika, from the Sanskrit, is said to be the source of the universe and creator of infinite worlds, the bringer of pleasure and pain and every human experience in between. Matrika is keeper of sound, speech, and all levels of conceptualization. Matrina chose to limit herself in human form in order to share her important message, a message of unconditional love.

Matrina explained that she and her six sisters ruled the very thing I was discovering...the subtle energies of words and constructs. While they had at first enjoyed the game they had created...very much at our expense, keeping us trapped within the illusion...they began to see it as limiting and debilitating. Matrina, one of the Seven Sisters, came to Earth as an act of compassion, to teach those with ears to hear. She wants us to know her, to understand her. She wants us to become the Masters and Creators of our dreams.

The purpose of her visits went deeper than simply getting me to think about sounds, words, and voice. The time I spent with her was like a download of sorts, a remembering of how to open to receive the many gifts that were awaiting me. Of course, it would take years for me to be able to hold their power.

"Let's start today by having you share what you've discovered about the letters so far."

I was, to say the least, a little embarrassed about sharing my puny understanding with what I now knew to be a Divine Being. I'd only had success with a handful of the alphabet so far. Some of the letters seemed more transparent than others. I grabbed my notes and stammered tentatively, "*A* is the first letter of the alphabet. *A* is equally rooted to heaven and earth." I looked at Matrina for encouragement to continue, her expression betraying no judgment. "It is the letter of prayer," I said with more confidence. "Utter *A* and you pray." Chills shot up my arms and my chest expanded with love as I went on, "*A* is pristine. *Amen. Alleluia. Allah. Apu. Abracadabra. Awaken!*"

"That is very, very good! Well done! Next?"

"*B* is the second letter of the alphabet. *B* is the Big Bang. It is the instantaneous, spontaneous presence." Something was happening as I spoke. I could feel the qualities rushing throughout my body like a niacin flush. This sure was a different kind of Vitamin B! "*B* is the *Belly* and *Birth. Beloved. Being. Balance.*"

Matrina nodded smiling, so I continued. I had about twelve letters completed so far, but at least a few notes for every letter. "*P* is the 16th letter of the alphabet. It is the power to prevail…to triumph over. *Pre* meaning before and *veil* being the veil of illusion. When we return to our pre-veil state, we automatically prevail. *Power. Path. Possibility. Pleasure. Prize. Peace.*" With each punch from the *P*, I was sitting up taller and feeling like I could lift an elephant.

"Very creative. Pre-veil," Matrina nodded her approval.

I glowed under the praise and continued until at last: "Z is the 26th and final letter of the alphabet. *Z* is the great leveler. It returns all back to *A*…the pristine and pure prayer, *Zen. Zero.*" I stopped and realized I was crying. "Matrina, what is this? What's happening? Why does this work bring tears to my eyes?"

"Let's try a meditation that I hope will help you answer that question for yourself."

I sat on my cushion and waited for Matrina to begin.

"We're going to imagine where you came from. Begin with the here and now, visualizing your body as it is. Place your attention on your whole form and breathe. Relax. Deeper and deeper, let go and fall into your body."

With each breath, I sunk deeper and deeper into myself.

"Now imagine a force beginning to build, a force both beautiful and powerful. Feel that force of Love building up inside of you so strongly that it blows you apart into millions of pieces."

I could see it...a million flecks floating above me like the candy bar in the original *Willie Wonka* movie when it's put through *Wonkavision,* a device that could shrink anything by breaking it apart into the teeniest of pieces, rematerializing it to fit inside the world of TV.

"Imagine all those pieces scattering, moving farther and farther apart from each other. When they spread far enough, you can no longer follow all the pieces with your attention. You can only follow one at a time. So do that, choose a piece to follow. See where it travels. Then put your attention on another, and then another."

I did so, my mind jumping from one fragment to the next.

"Each of those millions of pieces was once a part of you."

That was *me* expanding in a million different directions, but I could only focus on one little point at a time.

"Now step back; see all the pieces at once as having come from the whole that was you. Imagine them being pulled back into a unified whole. From millions of miles away, the pieces return."

The candy bar was reassembling.

"Now sit with your question."

I did. As I sat with the question about what this work was

about, I just let the images from the visualization drift and float in my mind's eye. Thoughts formed. Maybe everything was One, but we were blown apart into individual pieces that cannot attend to the whole. God split himself up to experience a million different perspectives, no one better or worse than the others, but all part of the One. Is the alphabet any different? Maybe it too came from the same One. Maybe the Voice of Life spoke for the first time and an explosion of sounds occurred. The alphabet is composed of just 26 individual pieces. Maybe they were once part of a greater whole. Maybe working with them consciously helps us remember who and what we truly are: mysteries.

Slowly, I opened my eyes. Matrina looked at me, expecting me to say something. I couldn't. My mind was a delightful blank.

"When you get your mind back, start working with the remaining letters of the alphabet." She smiled, patted my head like a puppy, and said she'd be back for more tomorrow.

₧₧

The next day, I was at my computer when Matrina came into the room.

"Matrina! Look. I found this website. A man in New Zealand has the alphabet all lined out with the energetic meanings for each letter." I thought I was off the homework hook.

"My, my. Look at that. He does indeed. I guess you can just use his list then."

"That's what I was think…"

"No! Have you learned nothing? That is one man's perspective. If you use his perspective, you lose your own. There's no harm in looking at what he's created, even adopting some of it. But don't forget to adapt it as necessary and completely leave behind anything that just doesn't ring true for you. Discern."

"You mean he's got some of it wrong?"

"He's completely right…for him, child. You are clinging to this idea that there is right and wrong, that there can only be one way. There are millions and billions of ways. Find your own."

With that, she was gone again. Matrina seemed a little upset with me…disappointed…losing patience. I couldn't blame her. I was rigidly attached to getting things right. I had this idea that if theories, or people, disagreed, one of them had to be wrong. Perhaps one of the greatest lessons Matrina finally did manage to get through my thick head was that right and wrong don't exist…not in the way I believed. At the same time, she was also teaching me to be less sensitive. Maybe her irritation had nothing to do with me. I resolved not to take it personally.

I looked back again at the website and began reading more detail. Interestingly, some of what I had gleaned from certain letters were corroborated on the page. But for others, there was no similarity at all. I decided Matrina was right. I had to do this on my own. It had to come from me. So I shut down the computer and went into meditation.

Three weeks later, I had reprogrammed every single letter of the alphabet. It was quite an accomplishment in such a short time. Of course, I knew this was just the beginning. I had merely put the map together, but I still had a long way to travel.

The 4th Gate: Bricks and Mortar

Whatever the reason for her mood the other day, Matrina was her old self today. After spending quite a bit of time working with the alphabet, she turned my attention back toward words.

"Nothing you say is inconsequential. Every utterance has importance in your experience of reality. Pythagoras, the Greek philosopher, trained his students in the mysteries of the voice and even used poetry to treat illness. This is the gateway to impeccability. You are ready for that responsibility now." She pulled something out of her bag. She had a way of doing that...sort of like Mary Poppins. "Here, I brought you something."

"A Harry Potter movie?"

She popped it into the player and used the remote to select a scene. In it, a novice of magic was having a terrible time asserting control over an unwieldy wand.

"Human beings are like that with words. We have this wand—this sword of speech—and we're a mess with it. We have to master our words in order for the Universe to respond to us in our desired manner. The Universe is programmable."

Even though I now knew who...what...she was, she still usually spoke of herself as "one of us," a human.

"Matrina, I knew someone who was very concerned with and aware of words. He constantly caught other people misusing their words...at least according to him: *You shouldn't say that. What does that mean?* It would drive me crazy."

"I'm not talking about getting hyper-critical here, and I'm definitely not suggesting you micromanage anyone else. I'm not asking anyone—including myself—to never say the wrong thing, whatever that means. I'm especially not asking anyone to beat himself up—or worse, say nothing at all for fear of getting it wrong. No, what we must do is forget the everyday meanings of certain strings of words. Instead, let's focus on tapping into the intelligence hidden within each letter and combination of letters in the words we speak. There's an intelligence far beyond comprehension. As you've now learned, each letter is actually a living organism with its own unique brand of wisdom, its own message. With intent, we can change even highly charged words like *nigger* or *fuck* into servants of higher truth."

"Yikes!" I was shocked to hear Matrina use such language.

"See that! That reaction you just had—to a couple of *words*!"

"Fair enough. I've given them power over me. But isn't there an element of respect for others to consider too?"

"Of course, we need to be respectful lest we put ourselves in uncomfortable or even dangerous situations needlessly. But once we know the truth—that words can't touch us or anyone else without an agreement—we can help diffuse them in the collective consciousness, and we can pull the plug on our own reactivity. Sooner or later, the butterfly's wings *will* create a hurricane."

"The butterfly effect, yes. Hey, I just remembered something. Years ago, I discovered that there was an energy-shifting power in uttering certain words. Whenever I felt off center, I'd repeat to myself: 'Peace. Joy. Wonder. Ocean. Fantastic. Dream. Wholeness. Gentle. Grace.' Whatever came to me. It was a step away from an affirmation in that it wasn't very specific. I wasn't saying a meaningful sentence. I wasn't using words in the realm of the mind. And I would shift states so gracefully with this practice that I very quickly felt at peace. I never realized what I was doing until now. I was tapping into the energetic essence of these words."

"What a sweet practice."

"Well, what I noticed just now is that I had a physiological response to the language you just used. I felt afraid. So if certain words can inspire, then other words can destroy and cause division, can't they?"

"Of course. But if you find yourself reacting to a word—like *fuck*, for example—then the best thing to do is clean it up for yourself so it becomes just another word. If you leave it entrenched in guilt or shame or punishment or whatever it evokes for you, it will always hold power over you. You don't necessarily need to clean up words like *peace* or *dream* or *grace*, though some people do, since those words were created to heal and instill calm. But words that were created to shock or demean, those need our help. It is our responsibility to alter their energetics, not to feed them even more of our superstition or negativity."

"You know, a few years back, I changed my name."

"What happened?"

"Something very strange...right in the middle of a performance. I was doing my thing on stage, singing in front of several hundred people, when suddenly a distinct voice in my head asked, 'What are you *doing*?' I'd never heard anything like it."

"What did you do?"

"Thankfully, the words of the song I was singing automatically continued to flow out of my mouth, but inside, in front of everyone and under hot lights, I was dissolving into a black hole of doubt."

"In what way?"

"Well, what *was* I doing? Was this a metaphor for my life...singing someone else's music, reciting someone else's lines? Those words echoed in my head." I swallowed hard remembering. "Somehow I made it through the show that night, but something irrevocable had taken place. I knew I was done with that life. If I was going to use my voice in this world, it was going to be *my* voice singing something...else. I didn't really know what that meant. I just knew it wasn't speculation."

"A gift of grace!"

"It didn't feel like a gift at the time. I was lost. I'd been performing my whole life. It was my identity. The name I had back then just carried so much of that old me, and I didn't feel like that person anymore. She died on stage that night."

"And that's why you changed your name?"

"Yes. At the time, I had just read a beautiful book called *The 5th Mountain* by Paulo Coelho. In it, he wrote about choosing a name that directs your life, like a beacon or compass. So that's what I did. And it has served me well ever since."

"How so?"

"Well, for one thing, it allowed me to detach energetically from my past. And it also helped me attach to what I wanted for myself…to live my life vibrantly, singing my own song. My name, Wrenne, became my reminder. And I hear that reminder constantly."

"Names are certainly extremely powerful. I know of a tribe that gives every child a song at birth. They sing that song if ever and whenever that child strays as well as upon death."

"You mean, if the child gets lost or something?"

"Yes, but lost in wrongdoing. Even as an adult. Names are like that. They call us home. Chanting someone's name or even just the vowels of our names can be a powerful healing tonic…"

Just then my phone rang.

"But we'll save that for another day."

೫ ಔ

That phone call turned out to be some rather disturbing news about a theatre friend in the hospital. He'd been in a hit and run accident while riding his bike. Since he was 2000 miles away, I felt a little helpless, but then I remembered what Matrina had said. Chanting a name can be a powerful tonic. So that's what I tried. I chanted Ethan's name, praying it could reach him and help. I imagined waves of sound washing over him in his hospital bed soothing his distress and reminding each cell of its healthy state.

When Matrina appeared the next day, I told her what I'd learned about my friend and what I'd done.

"He's such a good guy. He's got a family...a wife and two very small children...and I know times have been rough for them already. I feel so badly for them all. I didn't know what else to do."

"Good work, child! You did the right thing."

"I'll probably be a little distracted today, but I'll try to be in the moment. What's on our agenda?"

"I think you just gave it to me. There is a distinction between being 'in the moment' and really being 'in the Now.' The moment is already defined and filled with concepts—computer, hand, wind, tree, breath. Everything we experience for the most part has already been defined. The meaning for everything has already been determined before we even realize what it is. That's how fast the collective mind works. That's what we're up against."

"The collective mind?"

"Ask yourself, 'What is not mind?' Then watch yourself go nuts looking for it. It's like a dog chasing its tail. Everything you see, think, feel, interpret, and experience is mind. Right?"

I sort of nodded, not really knowing what she was saying. She wasn't looking at me anyway. Her voice took on a different tone: louder and more high-pitched.

"You'll feel like you can't get out of it. You'll roam from room to room, asking: 'Is this mind? This is mind. That is mind. Oh my God, it's all mind!' And then, you'll ask, 'Is it *all* mind?' Every which way you turn, you'll realize you're trapped within your own mind. And then you'll start to self-soothe, rocking back and forth like an autistic kid, slapping your fingers on the side of your head."

"I will?"

"Maybe."

"Matrina, you're nuts." But at least she had me smiling again. We were both quiet for a long moment. "I remember reading in a biography about Buckminster Fuller that at one time in his life, he didn't speak in an attempt to become completely impeccable with his words."

"What a beautiful and courageous act!"

"I'm so curious about how I express myself and whether the words I use are in line with my true nature."

"In the Bible and in numerous creation myths from cultures all over the world, it's written that the world began with the word. Nothing existed until it was named. Once named, we could identify it—tree, rock, sky. We could tell a bird from a dog. We could invent Velcro and write the *Declaration of Independence*. We could divide people with concepts like *us and them* or *good and evil*. Once things are named, we tend to forget that we are the ones who created them, and therefore, we are their creator. We come to believe that they are static, that they determine our reality, that they are, in fact, real. If our words create our reality, then what does our reality say about us? And more specifically, what does *your* reality say about *you*?"

"Looking back on my life, I know I've said things like, 'I can't live without chocolate,' or 'I'd die if so-and-so left me.' I told myself I wasn't capable of math and even things like: 'I'm so sick and tired.' I didn't know what I was doing. I was a creator who had forgotten she was creating."

"Yes, and with that hindsight, do you have a better sense of what you were actually doing?"

"I was shutting myself off to possibilities, I guess. I bought into, and therefore perpetuated, the myth that the past repeats itself. I was ensuring my continued anxiety with algebra, which incidentally, I went on to teach years later. I was literally making my body sick. I was scaring myself."

"When we speak unconsciously, we manifest unconsciously." Matrina paused and then continued in a new direction. "There are so many words whose time for extinction has come. In Bucky's case, he stated that there is no such thing as *up*. We live on a sphere called Earth. We are sticking out into space.

Therefore, there is only out and in. *Up* doesn't exist."

"As for me, I'd like to do away with *should*. What a nasty word! It immediately brings to mind I'm bad because I'm not meeting some expectation...or someone else is bad because they aren't meeting *my* expectations. Then there's the lovely word *afford*. What exactly does that mean?"

"Good one! Every time you hear yourself saying, 'I can't afford it,' you are practicing the worst form of black magic against yourself—a form that will surely make it so! And then there's war. How often do we hear that word these days? What impact is it having on our psyches? By reclaiming the power of the word, we can create something beautiful. What if, starting today, everyone wielded words with the utmost care? What if we stopped putting ourselves down? What if we stopped passing judgment? What if we used words like *compassion, forgiveness,* and *acceptance* in place of words like *hatred, resentment,* and *resistance*? Could ignorance and war exist in a world that had no symbols for such things? What if we focused on using words that could create the world we want instead of the one we believe in now?

"We are becoming—returning to—that which exists beyond thought. Words are tools. But rather than master these tools, words have become our master, defining us and our universe as if they were the power or the very thing to which they point. But the power is in the consciousness that creates the word, not in the word itself. Words themselves are empty, but for the tremendous power we grant them by placing our total and unquestioning faith in them. If we're going to change our own lives and life on this planet, it's essential to reclaim our faith from words and begin to master them as the tools God intended."

I just loved it when Matrina got wrapped up in a tangent like that. She called them her "rants." It wasn't so much *what* she said as *how* she said it. It was as if some force would overtake her, inspiring her expression. She would gesture emphatically with her graceful arms as if drawing the meaning up through the words themselves like a conductor of an orchestra appears to beacon music from his musicians.

"So next time, be ready for a grammar lesson."

"Are you kidding?"

"Oh, contraire! The parts of speech are significant seeds that shape our reality."

ℰℭ

I heard a car honking in my driveway. I wasn't expecting anyone, so I thought it might be for a neighbor. When I looked out the window, though, there was Matrina in a gorgeous midnight-blue Mustang convertible with creamy, leather upholstery. I didn't even know she could drive. She didn't seem to have much use for a car with all that popping in and out.

I grabbed my bag and ran out to her.

"Wicked car!" I said with admiration.

"Thanks! Jump in. We're going for a ride."

I got in and pulled the seatbelt on. Who knew what kind of driver she was?

"What do you know about adjectives?" she asked before I had even settled in.

"Adjectives are words we use to describe. *Amazing, stressful, unusual, green...*"

"Or *wicked*," Matrina added. "Adjectives represent our link to our inner judge, the voice that, at its best, can help us discern what to move towards and what to move away from and, at its worst, can fill us full of righteous hatred and superiority. The adjectives we use relate to the way we experience life. Are there adjectives you favor when describing church, money, racism, politics, or a loved one? Pick one."

"Well, when I think of church, I often think of hypocritical leaders, hierarchical structures, and long, boring sermons." I had

56

to yell now, as we entered the highway.

"What do you notice about your choice of descriptive words? Are they 'positive' or 'negative'?"

"Hmm…pretty negative."

"Just imagine the difference in how we feel if we say, 'That was a wonderful sermon,' instead of 'That sucked!' Forget for the moment that one may feel truer than the other. The question is, which feels better?"

"'That was a wonderful sermon,' of course."

"Exactly. So why not follow the trail that leaves you feeling better. Why even start down the road of 'that sucked.'"

"I don't know. Because sometimes, it really does suck?"

Matrina laughed. In her momentary distraction, a hasty driver cut her off, causing her to slam on the brakes. "Watch where you're going, you delightfully ignorant but none-the-less lovable miscreant!" she shouted, anger flashing in her eyes. She looked over at me, the anger gone, as she took our exit. "The adjectives we choose can diffuse our usual emotional charge and help us fend off an amygdala crisis."

"Amygda-what?"

"The amygdala is that part of the brain that controls fight or flight. It can cause us to react irrationally to a perceived threat. Maybe the threat is nothing more than a slight to our egos or salt in an old wound. If we don't realize this, we perceive the threat as an actual life-or-death challenge and act accordingly. It can be very self-destructive."

A few minutes later, we arrived at a park. Matrina grabbed a backpack from the backseat and off we went. We found a shady spot near a picnic table, and Matrina removed a sketchpad and markers from her backpack. I looked at the markers and then at her, but she wasn't giving up any secrets just yet.

"What's a noun?" she asked.

"Easy. It's a person, place, or thing."

"Yes, that's what we teach our children, but we do them a

great disservice when we fail to point out one important key."

"I'm listening."

"A noun merely *represents* a person, place, or thing: it is not the thing itself."

"That's right. I remember talking about that once before. Funny how easy that was to forget!"

"Just think how often we take the nouns we use for granted and assume we know all about something just because we can label it. She picked up a colorful stone. "Take this rock, for example. *Rock* is the name for the energetic pattern we call *rock*; it is not the rock itself. We can describe the word with adjectives in an attempt to know it, but calling it *hard, igneous,* or *red* means different things to different people. A blind man doesn't see red — unless he's angry. And someone else might prefer smooth stones to pointy ones and not find this one all that useful."

"I prefer sparkly ones myself."

"The point is, we can't take nouns for granite."

"Ha ha; very punny."

"Nouns play a very important role in maintaining the façade of our reality. Humans are noun-driven; we love labeling things. These little units of speech have the power to separate us from our experiences. If we can't label something, we say it is *problematic*. Because we *can* label something, we think we know it. Think how much better people tend to feel when a mysterious symptom is diagnosed. We use these labels like justifications, 'I can't do that because I have *ADD*.' Of course, *ADD* is a real condition that requires learning new strategies. That's not the point. Attention challenges require a change of approach to everyday tasks, period. The name *ADD* is just a label, a construct. And with every label comes an energetic signature unique to each individual, some highly emotional. Just think what the words *cancer* or *depression* trigger for you."

I didn't care for either of those words. I especially hated the word *depression*. I had been labeled depressed at different points in my life just because I wasn't all bubbly and smiling.

"What about the word *terrorist*? That one does all kinds of things to people."

"Good example. What pictures, people, and places immediately come to mind? Do you feel fear?"

"Not really. Not anymore. But I did at one time."

"Nouns can be used to divide and conquer. Let me give you some examples: *cat* or *dog*, *apple* or *orange*, *American* or *Terrorist*, *us* or *them*."

"Wow, nouns really do divide and conquer."

"It's worse than that. They can keep us deluded. I'm sure you've heard labels like *Lightworker*, *Indigo Child*, *Starseed*, and other New Age designations?"

"Yes. I have a lot of the characteristics ascribed to them."

"But you don't consider yourself to be one or the other?" she asked with obvious curiosity.

"Well, not really. I mean, in the end, we're all bigger mysteries than we could ever fathom."

"Good for you, child! Yet there are plenty of people out there who believe that one of these words is the entirety of what they are, that such a label defines them. Tell me, if you were certain you were a Starseed, would you bother to keep asking the question, "What am I really?"

"Probably not. I would think I already knew."

"And you'd think you knew that others weren't that if they didn't fit your idea. It's just more *us and them*, *black and white*, *yes and no*, *right and wrong*. Eternal duality. That's the best nouns have to offer us. They perpetuate illusion."

"So what can we do about it?"

"Imagine what it would be like to be an infant again. You wouldn't understand the separation between things. You wouldn't know that that face leaning toward you is *mother* and that that thing in your mouth is a *breast*. You merely sense with your senses a very pure experience uncorrupted by nouns.

Everything is connected. This is our natural state."

I tried to see things from the perspective of a baby.

"But it's so hard to imagine what life was like before I knew all these words!"

"Try an experiment. Get playful with nouns. Say you are 'taking your banana to the hospital for an audition' when you are taking your car in for service. When you pick up a pencil to jot something down, label the pencil *chimpanzee*. It's all relative. Shake up that concrete world we call reality."

"Calling a car a banana is the key to loosening the power nouns have over us?"

"Skeptical? Good! Well, focus on action instead. There's an old meditation trick of labeling everything you are doing as you are doing it. *Thinking, breathing, sweating, watching, thinking*. Let's look at the words that represent our actions."

"You mean verbs?"

"Yes, verbs are action words like *run, investigate, paint,* and *postulate*. Verbs are our link to 'being' in this world. And then there are adverbs and adverbial phrases that describe verbs and give us additional insight. *Slowly, joyfully, absent-mindedly,* and *vigorously* are all ways we do things."

"I heard someone once say that how we do anything is how we do everything. While I don't necessarily agree that how I chop vegetables is how I shave my legs, I get his point. If my desk at work is a complete disaster, chances are pretty good that my car or house is also a mess."

"Yes, adverbs are the key to our habits of doing. Let me ask you this. Don't answer. In fact, close your eyes and just dream. How do you accept disappointing news?"

I thought about that, but in typical Matrina fashion, she went on before I could answer.

"How do you communicate your needs and desires? How do you receive a compliment? Adverbs can reveal a lot about our state of mind as we begin to investigate the way we do things."

My mind began dreaming me in different situations in response to Matrina's questions. I saw myself in high school, losing a poster contest I had so desperately wanted to win. When the winner was announced, I begrudgingly accepted that it wasn't me. I cried bitterly in my room for hours afterwards, feeling cheated because the winner hadn't followed the rules. Then I remembered a time right out of college when someone told me I sang like an artist paints. It was high praise that felt oppressive under the weight of my self-doubt. I did everything I could to deflect the praise.

"And remember," Matrina continued, "we have a choice. There are plenty of adverbs, and we can try them all on. Which ones feel the best? Which ones add to our lives and give us peace? *Obsessively* or *gracefully*?"

I opened my eyes. I was beginning to feel overwhelmed by everything again and didn't think I could take much more today.

"Matrina, what are the art supplies for?"

"Art therapy. Let's have some fun!"

I remembered as a kid how happy a new box of fragrant crayons made me feel. All those colors! I'd select and combine those colors, watching my creation unfold on the page. It was like a meditation.

Matrina believed that creating art was a great way to help the body and mind integrate new information. She said colors were therapeutic in and of themselves, but that using them to create something new helped the imagination to expand. I could relate.

ಸಾ ೞ

A day later, Matrina entered the room humming. I recognized the tune from somewhere...an old jazz standard? I knew I'd heard it somewhere before. She seemed to be in an excellent mood, all decked out in mismatched animal prints with a bright orange and purple scarf on her head. Only she could make *that* work.

"Good morning! *If* you are ready to begin, today we'll talk about conjunctions. *But if* you aren't ready, we can just listen to music *and* eat ice cream."

"Conjunctions? Oh! That's what you were humming...that song from *School House Rock*! I used to sit through Saturday morning cartoons just so I could catch those. I hadn't heard that in forever."

"Today will be full of *ifs, ands,* and *buts*. Did you know these seemingly innocuous parts of speech pack a powerful little punch?"

"They don't strike me as terribly important, to be perfectly honest."

"Let's say your blind date says something like 'I like you, but...' Uh-oh. Here it comes, right?"

"Yeah, that *but* pretty much wipes out anything positive that may have come before it."

"Would you prefer he said something more like, 'I like you, and I never want to see you again?'"

I was thinking it rather depended on the guy, but Matrina continued.

"In this case, both statements remain true. The first part is not negated by, but rather joined with the latter part."

"So *but* tends to cancel things out, whereas *and* joins and unites?"

"Maybe that's obvious, yet how many times do we use these little words without realizing the full meaning behind them. 'He's a nice guy, but...', 'I'd love to help you out, but...' Clearly, he's not a nice guy in your opinion, and you wouldn't really like to help out at all! If words create our reality, what impact do our little *ifs, ands,* and *buts* have? 'I forgive you, but...' Doesn't that really mean, 'I don't forgive you?' Maybe what we really mean is: 'I would forgive you, but...' Or is it? How does it feel to say, 'I forgive you, and I'm still upset?' It's worth looking at."

"That's weird. It's like conjunctions are windows into our truth."

"What would happen *if* we all became more aware of the power in our words? There's that *if*. Although it be but little, it is fierce. How often do we decide what actions to take based on the mighty *if*? 'I can get that new car if my house sells.' 'If I get the new job, then I'll be so happy.'"

"But sometimes, asking *if* questions helps us, doesn't it? I mean, 'What if I suddenly had everything I ever wanted?' Asking that question helps me visualize what that could mean for me. It reveals possibilities."

"Good point. But remember, I'm not saying there's anything wrong with any parts of speech. I'm merely illuminating the traps. Nothing is all good or all bad."

I repeatedly and conveniently kept forgetting that I had nothing to defend with Matrina. She lived in a perpetual state of paradox beyond right and wrong.

"There's also *so* as in 'so what?' A good question to ask whenever something does not go according to plan. Do we accept what is or do we fight against it?"

"Hmm...so what?"

"*Yet*" is another doosie—as in 'not yet' or maybe 'and yet'— the former being a way of determining whether something is real for us in the moment and the latter being a means of second-guessing ourselves."

"So, what do I do with all of this? I'm starting to feel overwhelmed again."

"What if you didn't do anything? What if you simply allowed the knowledge to inform you on a level beyond the mind?"

"Are you saying I'm trying too hard?"

"Well, sure, most of the time. Really, all you have to do is just let it effortlessly sink into you. What I'm sharing doesn't really need to be memorized, regurgitated, or applied consciously. In fact, it's all just nonsense."

I nodded, having no clue what she meant.

"I know you're tired, but there's one more thing I want to cover today. Let the information just wash over you. This one is perhaps the most elusive, and I question myself whether to bring it up at all. But since you're starting to get sleepy, it's a good time to share it with you. Here it is: Prepositions are words that express relationship."

"Remind me; what's a preposition?"

"Prepositions are words that answer when, where, at what time, and those kinds of details—*without* for example. Does that word hold an emotional charge for you?"

"Interestingly, yes. My mind goes to the things I don't have. It goes to fear."

"There are other gems hiding within other prepositions. How about *according to*? How often have you given away your personal power or better judgment to some other authority? And *against* is a power-packed unit of meaning. What are you against? Who is against you? *Throughout* tends to hold a lot of personal history energy in it, as in 'throughout my life, this has been the case.'"

"My head is swimming."

"I've given you a lot to be with and think about." She handed me a two-page list of prepositions. "Your mission, should you choose to accept it, is to spend some time with these prepositions. You don't need to ponder each. Just work with the ones that speak to you. Maybe *beneath* holds a charge of judgment such as 'that is beneath me.' Maybe *away from* sparks emotional memories of loss from a move or fear from recollections of wanting to escape something. *Toward* might feel empowering if you relate it to moving toward a desired goal or may bring out hopelessness as you forever strive toward something unattainable."

"Hmm…this is going to take some time."

"You'll have it. Remember, we're simply drawing energy out of these little units of meaning. Use your breath to help you. As you come across a word with a charge, breath the energy you've spent on the word into the body. As you exhale, release the charge. This doesn't have to be something big or earth-shattering. It doesn't even have to make a whole lot of sense to the reasoning mind. Just get curious."

ℰↄ ℭℛ

It had been a nearly a month. I'd spent a great deal of my free time working with the various parts of speech and keeping notes in my journal. I felt eager for the next phase, but Matrina still hadn't returned. I know I was being ridiculous, but whenever she didn't show up for awhile, I would wonder if she'd found a much more worthy pupil. Just when I began to wonder if I'd ever see Matrina again, she popped in while I was grocery shopping.

"Matrina! I'm so glad to see you!" I gave her a big hug. "Aren't you afraid someone will see you do that…suddenly materialize out of thin air? You might make the deli guy question his sanity."

She looked over her shoulder toward the meat counter. "Not really. Even if he did see, it isn't likely his mind would accept it. He'd blink, maybe think he wasn't getting enough sleep. That's about it." She leaned over my shopping cart. "Say, you've really become conscious of what you eat."

"For the most part, I know what's good for me, bad for me, causes cancer, and helps me live longer, I guess. I definitely respect and honor my body more than I used to."

"And that is truly a wonderful thing. But what if I told you that no matter how careful you were at the grocery store, there's a really good chance you're still ingesting large amounts of poison every day?"

"What do you mean?"

"I'd like you to consider that language is a form of food and that we're feeding all day long, every day of the week. While we usually only eat food three meals a day, we are constantly grazing upon words—those we think, speak, and hear. Have you ever considered the impact that certain words, phrases, or thoughts have upon your energy, your creativity, and the overall quality of your life?"

"Since meeting you I have."

"Have you ever noticed how a few kind words from someone can linger like honey on the mind?"

"Well, sure. At least I think so."

We approached the bread aisle, which was barred by the carts of two women who were just hugging hello in greeting. Matrina motioned for me to pay attention.

One woman said to the other, "You look great!"

"Thanks, so do you. I hear Rita isn't doing so well, though. Have you seen her?"

"God, yes. She just looks awful. She must have gained fifty pounds."

"It's just horrible. You know, I heard that she's been drinking again, too."

"Another hospital stay is probably just around the corner," the first woman said, shaking her head.

"No doubt," the other agreed.

Matrina nudged me. "Have you ever paused to question whether listening to someone gossip really serves anybody? Or is it more like watching mold growing on bread?"

"I've never really enjoyed gossip. That conversation just reinforced that for me. How can they walk away from that conversation and not feel sick to their stomachs?"

"Ironically, they both think Rita is the one with the bad diet. They don't understand that gossip pollutes the very air around us."

I was ready to check out, so we headed to the front of the store. The cashier was cheerful and playful, if not downright harmlessly flirtatious. He asked how we were doing with a warm, genuine smile. He added that the raspberries were delicious, letting me know I'd made a good choice. He made ringing things up an art form. By the time we were outside, I was feeling lighter and happier and completely satisfied, and I said so.

"These experiences clue us into the nutritional value of our language. Awakening to the diet of our language can bring about great shifts in our mind, body, and spirit. We should give just as much attention to our diet of language as we do our diet of food."

"I agree. How do I start?"

"Well, you'll need to ask yourself what's on your menu. Start keeping track of what you are 'eating.' When you hear yourself saying, 'I can't do that' or 'I'm so sick of…,' it may go down nice and easy out of habit, but does it really taste good? If your thoughts to yourself were a food, would they be a super food like organic, vibrant, curly leaf spinach or an over-processed box of macaroni and cheese?"

I laughed. "Sometimes, they are a lot like arsenic. Anything else?"

"Go ahead and watch TV, but as you do, bring your awareness to it."

"I don't have a TV."

"Oh, that's right. Well, I know you watch stuff on the computer. What's the nutritional value of the language you hear? Are you watching a drama in which people are slinging insults and angry words back and forth? Are you tuning into scary stories?"

"I know I have a bad habit of reading about conspiracy theories and such. Sometimes, it actually depresses me."

"Why would you want to eat that? Why watch the news, getting all fired up about the latest political scandal? I bet you wouldn't eat that if it came on a plate! Bringing your attention to the passive activity of browsing will astound you. Begin to question whether what you are watching is of high enough quality to be considered nutritional or if it's just meaningless packaging that falsely proclaims 'all natural.'"

I wanted to defend myself for some reason, justifying my habits and choices.

"And may I remind you," Matrina continued, "that manure is all natural."

We put everything in my trunk and got into the car.

Putting on her seatbelt, Matrina said, "I want you to know something. I find you to be quite an insightful woman. I so enjoy your company."

This praise came out of nowhere. I held Matrina in such high regard that I was flabbergasted. I didn't know what to say.

"Are you always like that with receiving compliments? Choking on them? How often do you allow yourself to enjoy that high-cacao-content chocolate of a well-timed compliment? How often do you look in the mirror and say, 'Wow, I look beautiful today!'?"

I laughed at that, but a part of me felt sad. Maybe I need to acquire a taste for compliments...at least genuine ones.

After we got back to my place, we were putting away the groceries when Matrina picked up my carton of fresh-squeezed grapefruit juice. "A lot of people are just crazy about cleanses these days."

"Yes, I know. Juice fasts, colonics...some of those programs cost a small fortune."

"I suggest another kind of cleanse—one that won't cost you a dime or have you running for the nearest bathroom."

"Great! What is it?"

"Silence." I must have looked skeptical. "That's right. Take three days of silence and call me the next morning."

"Silence."

"Yes, silence."

"How can I possibly do that? I have to work. I have to communicate."

"Put a message on your answering machine that says, 'I'm on retreat. I'll call you back later.' When you need to communicate with others, write everything down. Suddenly, you'll have energy for a different kind of conversation, an inner one. *Why was I just going to say that? Was it important? Would it have helped or hindered the situation? I'm so angry; why am I having this reaction? Why do I feel like I'll burst if I don't share this! Wow, it's amazing how little I really need to speak.* Watch your awareness of language go through the roof."

"Okay, but now's not really a good time with work being so busy...you just wouldn't believe the mountain of work on my desk...and I have to work with clients by phone all the time. I have to talk. I couldn't possibly...I mean, I have to make a living, don't I? And with prices going up all the time..."

"Well, if not a silent retreat, then consider ways in which you tend to binge with words. Do you often exaggerate stories to manipulate or get reactions out of others?" She looked at me like I had just seconds ago been guilty of that. "Or perhaps you're more anorexic with words and tend to deny what's true for you as an avoidance mechanism. You may even find yourself downright toxic, spinning things to always make yourself look better, making excuses for your actions or inactions, ahem, and saying things to manipulate others. Or you may discover someone in your life is force-feeding you a load of bull, telling you what you can and can't do, or bringing you down with their words! Now, this isn't about beating yourself up for all the things you notice. Just observe without judgment. Once you see it, you can change your diet!"

"Anything else?"

"Yes, as a matter of fact. Celebrate Thanksgiving."

"But it's July."

"Doesn't matter. You won't need to cook a turkey with all the trimmings. This treat will be one of words. Express gratitude for all the blessings in your life. Be generous with those you love by offering words of encouragement and thanks. Be generous with yourself by showering yourself with kind thoughts and sweet expressions. Notice what language inspires you. Open up to receive the beauty of language—read poetry that stirs your heart. You may be shocked at what you discover."

"Matrina, have I expressed my gratitude to you for all you're sharing with me? I know I'm not always an easy person to work with. Thank you for your patience and for believing in me."

"You are so welcome, child. Now remember, this takes desire, courage, and self-discipline. If you think changing the foods you eat can be a great challenge, changing the words you use presents an even greater one. But the rewards are a healthy mind and a happy spirit to keep your beautiful, healthy body company. Now that's eating right!"

ℰℭ

By the next time Matrina made an appearance, I had actually summoned the discipline to do that silent retreat. It was unexpectedly wonderful...and much easier than I had anticipated. It sure did turn up the volume of the voice in my head, though. But that was a good thing. It gave me a chance to watch it in action...to study it without the usual distractions. I became aware of many of the things Matrina had spoken about. And I found myself becoming curious about not only the effect my words were having on me, but how they might be affecting others as well. That's when Matrina returned.

"Well, Wrenne, don't you look nice in those sweats!"

"Um...thanks, Matrina." There was something about her compliment that made me uncomfortable. I couldn't put my finger on it.

"Ever find yourself in a conversation with someone that left you feeling abused—only there was no evidence of any criticism or outward sign of judgment? Perhaps even a profession of love and respect?"

"I think I just did."

"Yes, because of what I said. 'Don't you look nice in those sweats' is actually the statement, 'You don't look nice in those sweats' phrased as a question."

"Oh, so that's why it felt more like a stab. It was."

She nudged me with her elbow to let me know she didn't mean anything by it.

"When someone says to you, 'I was merely expressing my opinion.' What does that imply?"

"I'm not sure I know what you mean. Doesn't it imply that the other person doesn't agree?"

"No, not quite. What I'm getting at is that there's an implication in the statement that you're being unreasonable. I could say, 'Every decision you've ever made turned out to be a mess,' and call that my opinion. But it's more than that. It's an accusation. Understand?"

"Can you give me another example?"

"You mean you *still* don't get it?"

"Ouch! Okay, so I'm a little slow."

"No, that was another example. If I were being impeccable, I could have stated the fact that you don't get it. What does *still* have to do with it? It implies something is wrong with you."

"Oh. Yes, I see that."

"So when someone tells you, 'You *certainly* sing well,' why might it rub you the wrong way?"

"Well, it's like they hold it against me or something. Like it makes them uncomfortable somehow, or they think that I think I'm a bigshot."

"Yes, and perhaps they wish they could do the same, but believe it's beyond them. It doesn't mean there's anything wrong with the word *certainly*. Just be aware. Stay conscious. Notice the emotional influence in the current of your statements."

I was quite proud of myself when the very next day at work,

I caught myself saying to a coworker that my boss *supposedly* put in a work order. With that one word, I was really expressing my frustration at her having dropped the ball so many times before. I had to admit, I was guilty of using little words like that to express my irritation and doubt from time to time.

℘ ℭ

Matrina told me to meet her at the library the following afternoon. I found her among the dusty stacks of reference books in the far back. She was sitting on the floor with an oversized dictionary on her lap. As I approached, she stood up and delivered into my hands the very heavy tome.

"How do we turn lead into gold?"

I stared at her blankly.

"Through the word. Reclaim your power over every word and rewrite it until every single words means love."

I took that as my next assignment and said incredulously, "You gotta be kidding me."

She ignored me and continued, "A large part of reclaiming our power of words is redefining what many of them mean to us. This happens on two levels. First, rather than accept a definition that brings us suffering or limitation, we can choose a new definition that empowers us. And more importantly, we can reclaim the energy of faith stored in certain words."

"Matrina, do you seriously expect me to do that with every word in this dictionary?"

"What?" She pretended not to know what I was thinking the whole time, pretended not to see a sweat breaking out on my brow. "Oh, no. That was just to freak you out."

"Mission accomplished."

"As I was saying—faith. Faith is stored in words. You need only listen to someone speak to know where his faith lies. You need only to hear a few words to know how he thinks and what he believes. But do you know where *your* faith lies? Are you aware of what *you* think and believe?" Matrina opened the dictionary and pointed to a word at random. "*Generosity*. What does that mean to you?"

"I think I see where you're going with this. For a long time, I always associated generosity with shame. I never felt generous enough because I couldn't measure up to my perceived definition, one that came from the eyes of others. My old definition of *generosity* went something like this: being generous is remembering people's birthdays and other special occasions; being generous is sharing everything you have with everyone, even if you don't have enough for yourself."

"And now?"

"Well, I've taken a great deal of pressure off myself. I guess now I would say that *generosity* is a natural and spontaneous act arising from the feeling of 'one's cup running over.'"

"So it's no longer something you have to force yourself to do regardless of your own circumstances. It's now an automatic response to an overflowing—of love, material goods, time, whatever."

"Yes."

"A New World dictionary is a necessity because we are entering a new world. As I've mentioned before, certain words and symbols are becoming obsolete. As creators, it's crucial that we pull our faith out of old concepts and place in them in redefined ones."

"Can you give me an example?"

"The laws of time are changing. These laws will break apart the egoistic concepts of *on time* and *late*. Everything is 'just in time.' Just—justice. Just in time, no sooner and no later than necessary for life's greater purpose. Just in time, so many words are becoming obsolete."

"You mean like *rotary phone*?"

"I'm talking about words like *want*. *Want* is a dying channel.

Want will soon be something referred to when talking of our history: 'It was a time of want.'"

I nodded. "So, what exactly am I supposed to do?"

"Just pay attention. Be curious about the words you use and the meaning they have for you—especially words that trigger an immediate reaction."

"Such as?"

"*Service.*"

"Oh, God. That's a good one. When I hear that word, I think of being sucked dry by others. Doing, doing, doing for others. So what you're saying is that I can change my idea of *service*. Service is not martyrdom. It's not about giving up what I love to do for what I feel I should do. It's not about forcing myself to do something. It's about simply being alive and available to the voice of God as She reveals my true desires."

"You quick like Ninja! Yes. Within those desires—your heartfelt desires—are true opportunities to serve. True service is an act of Love."

"I've never understood what that means until now. Service isn't about fighting with myself. True service comes from the heart, naturally. It feels good, in the flow, right."

"And another thing—we've done something terrible to *Love*. We've spiritualized it. We've contained it, analyzed it, measured it, exercised it, and destroyed it. *Love* is a completely corrupted symbol. Now anyone who utters the word and calls me to love is my enemy."

"Wow, Matrina. That's some pretty controversial stuff."

"'I love you.' 'If you loved me, you would…' 'I love chocolate.' 'I don't know how to love.' 'Do you love me?' 'I'll never love this way again.' 'Love your neighbor as yourself.' 'Love me forever and ever.' Love. A tiny word with a lot of muck covering up its power. I'm so happy that I don't understand Love, for if I did, I'm sure I'd have nothing but a sorry fragment of it, a little piece that I convinced myself was all it was or all it ever could be. Love is so much more than anything and everything. It is everywhere, in everyone, and in everything. But when we insist on defining it, Love naturally gets a bad rap. It becomes corny, pithy, overused, false, or too serious. But our ability to salvage Love, to mine it from the pile of garbage it's buried in, to shine it up and share it—that is our salvation. What if we became boundless vessels of Love, unafraid in every moment? What if our Love was so great that nothing but Love could exist in our presence? What if we stopped defining Love and instead let it be? I've heard people out there say some very mundane things about Love. They spout the generic, maybe simply because they want to have the experience and have yet to do so. Someone says, 'Tune into your heart and all will be well,' and people bow down and say, 'Guru!' I say, 'We already know that one. Tell us something we don't know!' May what I share with you never be generic!"

℘ ℛ

My New World dictionary was expanding. I had redefined forgiveness, depression, selfishness, and many other words that at one time had confused or confounded me. And better still, these new definitions were having an immediate impact on how I lived my life. It was somehow becoming easier to be true to myself. To celebrate, Matrina had offered to take me out to eat. We sat at a local vegetarian restaurant and talked, having just ordered enough food for three people. Matrina sure could pack it away. How did she stay so fit?

I looked around hoping to catch the eye of our waitress.

"Something the matter?"

"I don't have a fork."

"Oh." Matrina took a pen out of her purse, wrote something on a napkin, and handed it to me.

"Matrina, I can't eat with the word *fork*.

"That's right! And don't you forget it!"

I just counted that as another one of Matrina's weird lessons. I leaned over our booth to grab a fork...a real fork...from the table behind me and dug in.

"Matrina, how would you define *impeccability*?"

"Impeccability has to do with speaking our truth and using the force of our word in the direction of truth and love for ourselves. When we can speak from our center—our integrity, no matter what—we have mastered impeccable speech. There is plenty of resistance to being impeccable with our word. Inside, we have a caucus of internal voices. Outside, we have—"

"Everybody else's. So being impeccable with our word comes down to making choices that are most in line with who we are."

"More importantly, being impeccable with our word comes down to realizing who we are *not*. Don't let newfound awareness become a trap. It isn't something you want to build like a muscle, or practice like a yoga posture, or eventually you'll find yourself a slave to it. At some point, you just have to let go—into impeccability."

"But how?

"Find some 'guts.' Literally. Listen to your body, particularly to your gut. It knows. Part of speaking up is paying attention to its niggling. We're often so afraid of rejection, we don't even ask for the simplest of things. Even in our closest relationships, we actually expect the other to intuit our desires. It's ridiculous! Speaking up demands that we ask for what we truly want and say what we truly mean."

"I admit that not speaking up hasn't exactly been working for me."

"It means being bold enough to verify whether the assumptions you're operating on are actually true. That takes guts too and requires vulnerability. You'll be amazed at how dramatically your life can change just by learning to ask for what you want. Care to venture a guess on the two most powerful words in our language?"

"*Please* and *thanks*?"

"Good guess, but *yes* and *no*."

"Yes and no…you mean I'm partly right?"

"No, I mean, *yes* and *no* are the most powerful words in our language."

"Oh."

"Let's begin with the mighty *no*. The best *no* comes without justification from a place of being open, not closed off. How do you say *no*?"

"I'm embarrassed to say that I avoid the situation. I even avoid certain people so I don't have to say no."

"Sounds a little isolating. What if you learned to say what was true for you in all situations, no matter what?"

"I'd like to. Sometimes, I'm just not sure how."

"Get curious. Notice any impulse you have to justify yourself. Notice when you become rigid in a situation. Do you have difficulty saying no to someone in particular? Write down his name. What are the types of things or situations you have trouble saying no to? Write it all down."

I grabbed my fork, I mean, paper napkin…and Matrina's pen and started jotting things down. Matrina leaned over the napkin, trying to peak, and grinned.

"Care to share?"

"What, right now?"

"Why not? Just give me one example."

"Well, I sometimes have a hard time turning down invitations, especially if the other person seems genuinely excited."

"In that case, would you like to play a game with me?"

"Sure."

"You were supposed to say *no*."

"Oh. No, thank you."

"Interesting. You couldn't just say *no*. You added a *thank you*. Why?"

"Just trying to be polite, I guess."

"Are you sure?"

"Not with you looking at me like that." I thought about it. "I suppose I was probably more interested in maintaining my self image of a respectful person...maybe trying to make myself feel better."

Matrina stood up on her chair and loomed over me. "Wrenne," she began in a loud, stern voice, "get up and fetch me a menu!" She drew the attention of the entire restaurant. I felt mortified. She watched my reaction, then climbed down. "How did that change your reaction, feelings, and responses?"

"You mean aside from embarrassing the hell out of me? Well, having you tower over me like that was a little intimidating."

Just then, the waitress came over to check on us. She probably wondered if we'd be trouble. "Everything all right?" she asked.

"No," I said to be funny...you know...practicing my *no*. "I mean, yes, everything is fine."

She walked away, frowning, glancing back at us.

Matrina just sat there grinning. "Shall we continue?"

I said, "I would prefer not to."

"No, child, just say *no*."

"No."

"Like you own it."

"No!!!"

Now *I* had the attention of the entire restaurant. Oh, well.

"Okay, good. Maybe not so angry," she said chuckling. "You don't need to scare anybody. It's a *no* with love."

"No." I said it this time almost without thinking about it. It felt so natural and undefended.

"How did that feel?"

"Surprisingly good. I think I like the idea of not having to explain myself. In fact, I think I just realized for the first time in my life that *no* is actually enough!"

"Congratulations! With practice, you'll discover more and more about how manipulation happens around our inabilities to use these two little words clearly and without justification. How about *yes*? When do you have a difficult time using this word?"

"When I really want the person I'm with to pay the tab?"

"Ha ha. Gotcha covered. In what ways is saying *yes* different than saying *no*?"

"Maybe it stems from a belief that I don't deserve something."

"That's likely. Let's try something. I'm going to call out a list of things. Take a moment between each one to close your eyes and feel the statement. If it resonates with your desires, say *yes*. Say it openly and fearlessly. See how it feels. Notice if there are any underlying currents in your feelings that point to a deeper contradictory belief. Ready?"

"No...just kidding."

"I've created a monster. Okay, first one—fulfilling work full of creative projects."

"Yes!"

"Complete faith in the laws of abundance."

"Yes. Wait, I said *yes*, but I struggle with that from time to time. It doesn't feel truthful to say *yes*."

"Honey, do you want complete faith in the laws of abundance?"

"Yes!"

"Then don't doubt yourself out of it. So, how about a romantic and sexy love affair?"

"Yes?"

"Hmm. Travel around the world?"

"Ooo, yes!"

"That one was easy? Why?"

"Ah, I have no doubt about that. I really do want to travel the world."

Just then, the waitress popped over. "Dessert?" she asked, to which we both enthusiastically replied, "Yes!"

The 5th Gate: Tell Me a Story

I remember sitting in a meditation group once with some friends, and a woman spoke of her desire to embody her highest self. She lifted her arms to the ceiling and looked up. I watched her and listened to her speak…and then gasped when I realized she was making a grave assumption with her symbols. What I realized even then was that this woman assumed her higher self was 'out there' somewhere. She assumed she didn't already embody this self. But how could she not? And if she didn't already, how would she ever? I wanted to grab her arms and cross them over her heart and say, "Here. Now."

We speak like this all the time, often unconsciously. We project everything out in front of us or into the future, but if we really want to empower ourselves, if we really want to take responsibility for our own lives and our own personal growth, heaven help us, we must come to realize what we're doing. It seemed Matrina's teachings were really sinking in.

A similar thing happened recently. During a sweat lodge, the facilitator shared a tale of a Being to whom his ancestors prayed for help. The prayer was something akin to "We are such unwise and wretched humans. We need you to help us." And I thought, "What!?" We haven't the time to pray like that anymore. Maybe we needed that at one time, but not now. Now we have to save ourselves! We need to take our power and embrace our own ability to be warrior-like with our addictions and weaknesses. We must realize we don't need that kind of help…the kind afforded to powerless victims. We could certainly use the kind of help that comes to those already in their power…that of faith, courage, and strength. And we can always use the watchful protection of the unseen forces that respect, love, and serve us.

Matrina referred to this careful languaging of our stories as the art of storytelling. "We've all been writing fairytales since we were born. Your life has been a fairytale, filled with dark and foreboding characters, fairy godmothers, magical animals, princes, and princesses."

"And frogs."

Matrina ignored me. "And they really do come true. Look around you. Everything you see, the people in your life, the objects—they are the direct result of your fairytale writing. Let me tell you a secret."

I bent near.

"If we could just change our stories, make them kinder, gentler—more benign, at least—the world would change." Matrina let that sink in. "Do you like what you see? Or is it time to change your story?"

"Wait. Are you saying that how we tell our life story *becomes* our life story?"

"Yes! Think about it. Remember your Derrida? There is no 'outside the text' because there is only ever 'in context.' Everything we think we know is text; we're stuck in our own books! So the best thing to do is to rewrite the fairytales we're stuck in. Try telling your stories in new ways. If you tend to hide your emotions, tell a story with utter histrionics. Go way overboard, swooning and overemphasizing how important it all is. See how it feels. Or if your pattern is drama, try telling your story from the doldrums. Yawn. Nothing has color. Nothing is important. It's Eyore on hormones. Or go for the machismo. Be tight and rushed and very self-important. Try on for size what it would be like to live in a manner you're not accustomed to. After all, *you* are just a story."

"But if it's all just a story, what's the point of changing anything…if it isn't important?"

"Fact is, if it's a story, then it's an art. Don't neglect your art, Wrenne. Write the most beautiful story you can. Leave out the view that it's 'inconsequential.' That's no better than seeing everything as personal and important. If you have to have a story, make it a really, really juicy one you love and enjoy."

"Once I do all that, then what do I do?"

"Hopefully, you'll start to appreciate the choices at your disposal. We tend to react according to our habits and ingrained traits. Begin to realize that as a player upon the stage, you can play your role any way you like!"

A Fairytale

East of the sun and west of the moon, a shooting star once fell upon the earth. And from its mother's womb, a baby girl was born in late September. And her mother said, "You are my last rose of summer. I have a very special feeling about you, little one. You are going to do something important."

And so the child grew, delighting in singing, in playing with stuffed animals, and in all manner of games that exercised her enormous imagination. Most of all, she loved to dance. When she danced, she felt free...like she could fly.

Peter Pan was her favorite story. She set up a Neverland in her closet, where she spent hours hiding in an imaginary world of pirates, fairies, and mermaids. Her older sister knew the importance of her belief in magic, so she wrote small notes from Tinkerbell and sprinkled them with "fairydust." So the little girl's faith in magic was well-cultivated, as she was certain those notes really were from Tink. How wonderful that Tink knew about her and her Neverland closet!

The little girl had a pop-up book with pictures of Peter Pan flying over London at night. She believed that, just as the popstars on the record player were actually inside the device, the secret to Peter Pan's ability to fly was hidden somewhere within the pop-up mechanism of the book. She wanted more than anything to fly!

Despite her best intentions to "never grow up," she eventually did. As she grew older, she learned to carefully bury her fairy world beneath a very serious mask. She mastered perfectionism, criticism, and many other "isms" over time. Until one day, sad and weary, she looked in the mirror and didn't recognize herself. All that remained was that mask.

Thus began her journey back to Neverland. In her quest, she met wonderful teachers. One in particular handed back the powerstick she had just made and chuckled, "I don't know what this means, but this stick will help you become Peter Pan...whatever that means to you."

That evening, as she stood high atop a hill in the desert, within a medicine wheel, inside a circle of her Toltec warrior comrades, each with their powersticks pointing toward the setting sun, the wind began to blow. It blew so fiercely, the woman had to lean into it. As she yelped in joy and amazement, she spread her arms like wings and she was suddenly flying! She was finally free!

℘ ℞

Matrina and I had kicked back in my apartment, enjoying some iced chai. She had a habit of drinking from a glass with her little pinky extended. Today it made me chuckle. I shared a couple of stories from my life that I had rewritten, feeling that I was becoming a much better storyteller...maybe not as dramatic, but definitely kinder.

"You've certainly come a long way with your awareness of letters and words," Matrina praised me. "So let's go deeper. The voice has always been known to be a powerful healer."

I felt excited, like I was graduating into something new.

Matrina watched me settle deeper into my chair. "What if," she began, "what if every word you ever spoke was recorded somewhere?"

"I think that would make me a little nervous. I've said some pretty stupid, ruthless things in my time."

"When you consider what you've said over your lifetime so far, about yourself and others, are you filled with peace or a sense of regret or embarrassment?"

"Well, I'd have to say that at least my odds are continually improving. Thanks to you, I think I can die with peace. Fortunately, no one's been keeping a record."

"Think not? There's a theory called *Eternal Fade* that says a word once spoken is never lost. To illustrate how this works, imagine we play a tone and use a small amplifier to project the sound. At a certain point, we'd no longer hear the tone ringing in our ears, yet we could still hear it through the amplifier. What if we repeat the experiment, only this time with a more powerful amplifier? Again, our ears at some point cease to hear the tone. Then at another point, the small amplifier also goes silent. But the more powerful amplifier continues to carry the sound. If we were to use progressively stronger amplifiers and continue this experiment in the same fashion ad infinitum, when would the sound ever really die?"

"Uh-oh."

"This theory means that the words we speak are no small matter. And just think how saturated our environment is — carpets, furniture, the very walls — all soaked with thousands of conversations over the years. The signatures of all the words we've spoken lurk in the very air around us."

"But how do we get others to realize this?"

"We can't control the words others use. We never will. We have to remove the charge from their words when they land in us. Words work by hooking our attention. When it comes to the spoken word, fortunately, we tend to be selective about what we hear. If we weren't, we'd have so much information coming at us, we'd be in a perpetually overwhelmed state. It's only because we attach to certain words and not everything that *something* penetrates our attention."

"I think I've experienced that. I remember being upset by

what someone said or by a particular news story on the radio, and yet a friend had no reaction whatsoever to the exact same thing."

"It isn't the spoken word alone that holds power. The unspoken words in our own mind vie for our attention as well. In fact, they are the real trigger."

"I recently had an experience with that, too. Mind if I share it?"

"Please."

"I woke up with the thought: 'This is going to be a bad day.' Then I noticed how I got hooked by that thought all day long. As soon as I got up, everything started going wrong. I dropped my glass of water all over my papers. That made me late. I nearly got in a car accident. And I when I got to work, someone had left me a big mess to clean up. It truly was a bad day."

"You've discovered selective evidence gathering. You caught yourself collecting evidence to support your thought. This is something we do that's fueled by our need to be right. Congratulations on actually having the wits to see it in action! What you didn't see—or notice—was that you spilled water, not coffee, and that you didn't actually get into that car wreck. See?"

"Well, it's certainly clear to me that if we can become more aware of the impact of our words...both on ourselves and on others...we can begin to reclaim a lot of lost energy and power. What can I do to help build my awareness around this?"

"For starters, whenever you wake up with a thought like that one again, notice it and change it immediately! In fact, if you can catch yourself before the first thought of the day enters your head, you can choose the thought instead of having the thought choose you."

The 6th Gate: Do You Hear What I Hear

After rewriting many of the life stories with which I most identified, I came to understand the power in telling them from a new perspective. In stories where I was the victim, I changed the facts to make myself the hero. In stories where the villain triumphed, I created new outcomes with happy endings for all concerned. In essence, I was rewriting my life, and my attachments to old beliefs and points of view were evaporating.

I didn't realize the impact this work was having on my life until I ran into someone that I dated in college who had deeply hurt me. When I saw him, the story came rushing back and my mind began telling me how much I'd been betrayed and abused. In the next second, as I breathed and observed myself, I realized none of it was true. I wasn't hurt. I was fine. He was just a character in a story. Every ill feeling I'd held toward him lifted. It was miraculous. I was free!

Matrina and I sat on the floor in my apartment, going through her magical music collection…what seemed like a thousand CDs that she kept pulling out of her bottomless handbag. Matrina kept adding to a pile of discs she wanted me to listen to. It was like a big stack of pancakes, and I began to wonder if maybe her eyes weren't bigger than my stomach.

"If you listen, really listen, with your ears wide and every bone and cell in your body alert and attentive, you begin to hear beyond the music to that underlying presence that pervades existence. Open wide the ears of your heart!"

I liked this new direction that Matrina's teachings were taking. It felt mystical and mysterious.

"You begin to hear beyond words, beyond meanings and concepts, to the pure expression of Life—coming out of the lips of a laughing child, a gossiping coworker, or a preaching minister. You begin to hear the elements as they are expressed in every individual. You will hear one with watery tones, another evoking earth, and still another with a powerful fire-air combination that sounds like combustion. Did you know that the ears are one of the first organs to develop and that hearing generally is the last of our senses to leave us?"

"No, I didn't. Hearing must play quite a crucial role in our survival."

"Sound isn't processed through the mind, as are stimuli through our other senses. The vibration of sound impacts the body immediately. In fact, we don't only hear through our ears. Our entire bodies are resonance chambers; our very bones are perceptive of and receptive to vibration. To believe we hear only with our ears—or sing only with our voice boxes for that matter—limits not only our experience, but our ability as well. It makes us even more vulnerable to the force of *entrainment*."

"What's that?"

"To understand entrainment, at least for now, think about how you tap your foot to music. You just can't help yourself. Am I right? A stronger force always overtakes a weaker force. Lower vibrations always lock into higher vibrations."

"So, it's like getting caught up in the music?"

"Or any other vibration. Even emotion. If we entrain to something without free will, then we haven't really been listening or paying attention. We're simply passively hearing. Have you ever seen a snake charmer?"

"You mean those turban-wearing flute players with the snake in the basket?"

"Yes. Think about it. Here's this deadly snake forgetting itself completely, entranced, seduced into a dance by a beautiful melody. In a moment, just like the cobra, we too can forget ourselves and become enchanted—or even disenchanted—by music. The question is: who's doing the enchanting and why? Do they have our best interest at heart? Or are they merely out to sell us something, keep us subdued, or take our minds off the inner work we need to do?"

"Do music and sound always have an effect on us? Are we always vulnerable?"

I'd been drying a load of clothes in the drier, and it buzzed to let me know the clothes were dry, making us both jump. Then it shut itself off. I hadn't even realized the noise it had been making while we talked. The sudden silence was deafening.

Matrina cleared her throat with a smile. "Yes. Just because we get used to a grating noise in our environment doesn't mean it isn't irritating. It just means we have entrained to it. We may not realize that our nervous system is being bombarded with sound because we don't pay attention to most of it. How can we when there is so much sound around us all the time? It would impossible to process it all if we were fully aware and not selective in our hearing."

"From singing, I know that it's through listening that I'm able to create harmony, a beautiful and peaceful blending of two energies. If I don't listen, I can't harmonize. How do we learn to really listen...with our whole bodies, as you say?"

"It begins with awareness of all the sounds that exist in any given moment. We put aside our selective deafness and take in the whole story just as it is. This takes will power. We have to be willing to hear. As we grow our awareness, we can begin to hear the unique voices of individuals, animals, and instruments. Only then can we become better equipped to really hear sound. Once we're in a fuller relationship with all sound, we can use the full expanse of our own unique vocal palette. We become thrilled to blend our voices with one another. We learn to obey what we hear."

"What do you mean?"

"There is a group that I've been waiting to introduce you to. There, you'll learn more about listening than I could ever teach you by myself."

Matrina grabbed my hand quite abruptly, and we were

suddenly in a geodesic dome with a group of twenty or so others. I don't know how she did it. I felt like Scrooge in Dickens' *Christmas Carol*, being involuntarily dragged around the past, present, and future by ghostly visitors.

"Whoa!"

"This is a toning circle," Matrina explained, as if the miracle had not just occurred.

"What the f...udge just happened!"

"You must be dreaming," she said in a rather suggestive, hypnotic way that brought me into complete acceptance.

I looked around at the group sitting in the circle. Everyone's eyes were closed, and they were singing strangely...not with words or melodies, but with random vowels at different pitches.

"What are they doing?"

"They're toning. Listen."

I listened as one person sang an *OM* tone, another sang an *OO*, and yet another sang a rather clashing *EE*. Then a fourth voice joined in with a harmonious *AH*, creating a very pleasing chord.

Then the man before me opened his eyes and looked right at me. I didn't know how to explain my presence...heck, I didn't even know how I got here...so I just gave him a little wave. He didn't respond. "Can't they see us?" I whispered.

"No need to whisper," Matrina said in her normal tone of voice. "They can't see us or hear us. Tell me, what do you hear?"

"Well, I'm not sure *what* I hear. This is wild. They're all just doing their own thing. Occasionally, I hear something that sounds like music...like that!" At that moment, the group all entered into the most beautiful chord structure I ever heard. It was like hearing angels sing.

"Toning is like that. Sometimes, it sounds quite dissonant. Everyone is focused on him- or herself. Then, there are times when the group listens to one another—and something magical springs forth. It's all about patience, trust, being in the moment, and paying attention."

Something was changing within the group again...another shift. A woman on one side of the circle started to make a sound that someone across from her echoed. A third voice made a variation. Soon, everyone was playing with that variation. It sounded so cool. They were all smiling and obviously having fun, some waiting for the perfect moment to jump in.

"Ah, see, they just deepened their listening. You heard what just happened?"

I nodded.

Matrina went on. "At some point, we aren't just hearing, but allowing sound to carry us in its stream to other emotional states and states of consciousness. Our hearing—and our understanding—expand and refine until we journey further into other dimensions. That begins the process of transformation through sound."

At the time, I'm quite sure I had no idea what she was talking about. She spoke of sound as a living energy with its own intelligence. When we honor it, she said, we step out of its way and allow it full expression. We no longer try to control how things sound. It didn't make sense.

"As a vocalist," I protested, "I'm always trying to control how I sound. Isn't that necessary to sing well?"

"I'm not saying control is bad. I'm just saying it isn't all there is. We become better singers and better musicians when we open ourselves as wide channels to the living energy of sound—when we learn to hear *its* voice."

"So music is...speaking to us?"

"Music, Spirit, the Great Mystery—whatever you call it—is always speaking to us. Learning to really listen means waking up to this fact and taking in the guidance that is always with us. Then and only then can it also speak *through* us. Then we can sing without singing."

"This is all so exciting, Matrina."

ॐ ॐ

Despite the extraordinary experiences I was having with Matrina, the mundane details and responsibilities of my life still needed to be tended. This morning, I was bringing my car in for a brake inspection when Matrina popped into the seat next to me. I swerved and nearly hit a telephone pole.

"Must you do that?"

"Sorry. I thought you'd be used to it by now."

"I'm not sure I'll ever get used to it."

"Where are we going?"

"Time for my brake service."

When we arrived, I handed my keys to the desk manager, and Matrina and I sat in the waiting room with several other people reading magazines. Cable news blared from a television in the corner. Matrina looked around and then asked if anyone was watching TV. They all shook their heads, so Matrina got up and turned it off. The room plunged into silence. It suddenly felt much calmer. Everyone was obviously thankful, which struck me as odd.

"If no one wanted to watch that, why didn't they just turn it off themselves?"

"No one ever thinks to ask, do they? We just accept that we have to be assaulted by sound everywhere we go. Restaurants, airports, bars, even hospitals. It's a sickness. At least this place isn't piping in music at the same time."

A half hour later, the manager came over with a poker-face expression to tell me that my brakes should probably be replaced since they only had 30% of life left in them.

I was about to tell him to go ahead when Matrina said, "Let's talk it over."

The manager gave us some space, and I questioned Matrina.

"What's going on? I just as soon get it over with."

"He's lying." She sounded very matter of fact. There wasn't a hint of accusation or judgment.

"What?"

"He's exaggerating or something."

"How can you know that?"

"How do you think? Investigate."

This was awkward. I walked back to the manager and told him I wanted to think about it. He gave me my paperwork and had the car driven around.

When we got in, I handed Matrina the paperwork. Looking it over, she exclaimed, "See here. The technician marked the brakes at 40% tread. That's almost half the life left. By calling it 30%, the manager assumed he had a better shot at making the sale."

"Unbelievable. Where do these people get off?"

"Don't be surprised. It's their business to make money. It wasn't that far from the truth really, but far enough to tip the scales in their favor."

I wanted to go back there. I wanted to call the guy on his lie.

Matrina stopped me. "My take is, it was so close to the truth that he wouldn't even believe he had lied. He'd just say it wasn't that much of a difference. Let it go. Instead, work on your ability to detect truth from fiction within yourself."

I thought about that for a moment. "You just saved me a lot of money. I want to be a human lie detector too!"

"You already are, when you care to pay attention. You know when something resonates with you or not. When we only hear the surface value of sounds or even words, we're missing so much of what's being said on subtler levels. We deny our intuition. Think back. When he said you needed new brakes, what did you notice?"

I paused before answering. "Well, first I reacted to the fact that I needed to spend money. I wasn't very excited about that. But then I thought about my safety."

"And beyond that?"

"I'm not sure what you mean."

"There's the surface level of listening to which we're all attuned. For example, there is the actual statement, 'You are going to need new brakes.' We hear the vowels and consonants express the symbols *need* and *brakes*. But if you really listened, you would have noticed that the person saying those words did so in such a way that something in you didn't resonate with it."

I thought back. Interestingly enough, I did have a gut reaction when he said I'd need brakes. Something in me did know it wasn't right. I just didn't know what, so the feeling was easy to dismiss.

Matrina noticed the expression on my face and knew what I was thinking. "This subtle level of listening is what reveals incongruence."

"Incongruence? What's that?"

"Incongruence has to do with speaking in such a way as to hide either our personal truth or the actual facts. We say we like someone's cooking when really we find it tasteless. We agree to do a favor for someone when really we don't have time and resent being asked."

"I would never do that!" I joked, looking the other way.

"In this case, the mechanic exaggerated something in his favor—the percentage of life left on your brakes."

"Okay, I got it."

"Part of overcoming the confusion of incongruence is learning to trust ourselves. To do that, we have to let go of the ideas we have about ourselves. We have to forget the way we wish things were and face up to the reality of things. We need an inner strength and clarity to both be honest and maintain our boundaries, even if it means we'll no longer be seen as nice or smart, for example. Even if it means we'll 'lose the sale.' If you were paying better attention, you would have heard it too. From there, you could have listened even deeper to hear his motivation behind the lie. We learn to discern through sound."

"I had no idea there was so much more to listening than just hearing! That guy sure twisted the facts. What a lying son of a bitch!"

"Whoa, child! Pull up! Ease up on the judgment. There's really no such thing as facts—in the end, there are only agreements. So, if you don't agree, then it isn't true for you. But everything is a lie. The only thing the mind can manufacture is lies. Lies can, on occasion, land pretty close to the Truth, but let's face it—the Truth is out of reach of the mind. Even everything I've shared with you is one step removed from what I'm really pointing at. Until we wake up, we do the best we can, you see?"

"Well, okay, I understand that on one level. It goes back to storytelling, I guess. But how can I tell if, for example, a political figure is telling the truth or not. I mean, they rarely do, but why can't we ever just get them to admit it? Catch them in it?"

"The Politician is an archetype from which none of us are immune so long as we believe what we think. They agree with their lies. That's enough to make them think they aren't lying. The only way to bring light back to politics is for each politician to realize that everything is a lie—or at best, an approximation of the truth."

"I'm not entirely sure, but did you just call me a liar?"

"Of course you are! But there's no right or wrong implied here. No need to feel guilty about it, love. It's just the nature of being human. We make up stories. When the majority of people believe the stories, we have what we call 'shared truth' or fact. It still has nothing to do with ultimate reality. When you wake to the fact that you're lying all the time—or to put it in perhaps a gentler way, telling stories—you free yourself from needing to be right. You free yourself from fundamentalism, from the very stories you tell. It's an open door into freedom. It's lie-detecting at its best. I know you won't understand this yet, but beyond the idea of needing new brakes, there is also a soundless void beyond form where you, the mechanic, and the car all become completely meaningless. Even the 'plain facts' can't withstand the full light of

Truth."

That bent my mind considerably. Was there no end to this rabbit hole?

Matrina continued. "Information bubbles up from silent knowledge—what your Toltec friends call the *Nagual*. Then it enters consciousness in search of a bridge through which it can be expressed materially."

"I don't get it. A bridge?"

"Yes. Someone to relay the message. It's expressed through that bridge either with integrity or not, to some degree. Then it's received through the filters of those listening.

"So the message isn't always received as intended?"

Matrina snorted. "To put it mildly. People tend to hear—and communicate—according to their personal style."

"Personal style?"

"Sure. You probably know some people who say things like, 'I see what you mean.' Others might say, 'I hear you.' And some probably say something more along the lines of 'That feels good to me.' You might even know a few who seem to be in a constant state of poetic revelation."

"Well, I thought I was following you, but I'm not sure what you mean by 'poetic revelation.'"

"I'm referring to people who are in touch with Truth. Masters and Zen teachers often speak like this. But so can the gas station attendant. They are prophets who communicate through symbols at times when we most need to receive their messages. We don't always understand them, though."

"Okay, I get it now. I've experienced that from time to time."

"The thing is, when the world around us doesn't communicate in our style, communication becomes rather tricky."

"So if a person is born into a family that doesn't favor her communication style, she grows up feeling misunderstood?"

"I take it that question comes from personal experience?" I nodded, and Matrina continued. "It's likely. And you may have altered your natural inclinations so much, you no longer know what style you're most naturally inclined toward. Instead, you just have a feeling that it's so very difficult to communicate."

"Wow, that explains so much!"

"For example, a visual girl who grows up in a family where another style of communication is dominant may feel her survival threatened when beauty and order are not respected. Whereas auditory people just love to tell and hear stories, so they might get angry when things are obviously not being said. And then there are the feeling types who need to act things out—to touch and play. Because they are so dependent upon the body to feel, they may be perceived as airheads if they aren't supported to be well-grounded. Receiving communication that matches our style is a form of nourishment for the nervous system."

"So what style is the best?" I already knew this was a stupid question the moment it left my lips.

"No style is better than the other. They're all valuable, all beautiful. To some extent, we all express through each of them at different times."

"I was just going to ask you about that, because I can see myself as having more than one style."

"That's primarily adaptive—a matter of survival. See if you can identify the one that comes most naturally to you."

I spent time the following weeks learning to listen for people's communication styles, keeping the words they used as secondary. When I was able to connect in that way, it was amazing how easy it was to understand them, despite the words they chose. It was as if a window had been opened for me. I began to see so much beauty in the stories people told. I also began to honor what I now understood was my natural inclination toward the feeling style.

ഇ ⊂ഃ

When I woke up the following morning, I went through my usual routine of checking email. Something was waiting for me from Matrina; I didn't even know she *had* an email address. She had sent me three links to videos to watch.

I clicked on the first link. In it, an attractive blonde woman with feathers in her hair talked about the importance of our connection to the earth. She spouted some very basic spiritual principles...but the more she spoke, the more agitated I became. I felt uncomfortable, like I was tied down or something. I kept listening, though, because I figured if Matrina had asked me to watch it, it must hold some value.

As the video went on, I had thoughts like, "This woman doesn't know what she's talking about." I continued to listen, although I had left my computer. I did some work around the house, with one ear tuned to the interview. I kept feeling weaker and weaker for some reason. It was crazy! I finally cried out, "This woman is an idiot!" and returned to the computer to click off the video. I thought to myself, "Matrina, what on earth did you see in that?"

I went to video number two. The topic was something close to my heart...communication. A man shared his views about enlightened interaction, and I found myself looking forward to what he had to say. As the video progressed, I started to feel a twisting in my gut like a fist inside was trying to punch out. Still, I was determined to hear what he had to say. I didn't want to feel like I was being judgmental of both speakers so far, so I continued listening.

At one point in the video, a woman in the audience tried to ask a question. The speaker cut her off mid-sentence and went into a rant. My eyes bulged out in astonishment. I felt assaulted. As I watched...I had stopped listening at that point...I began to see the speaker's arrogance. He thought he knew it all. He thought he had it all together. I saw through his façade. It felt like his ego was directing his entire communication. "What an egomaniac!" I said to no one but myself. Did Matrina expect me to find some value in this? I no longer cared. I turned this one off too.

By this time, I had very low hopes for video number three. "Oh great. Another guru," was my thought as a man sitting on some kind of platform began speaking to a crowd. He looked rather humble and plainly dressed, which in itself was refreshing after the last video. As he spoke, my entire body started to tingle. He talked about getting a flat tire. It wasn't anything important; it was ordinary and yet filled with spiritual truths. The tone of his voice and his personal vibration penetrated me, parting the clouds in my inner sky. The more he spoke, the happier I became. I wanted to drink in his every word like pure crystal clean water. This man got it. He was the real deal. He was enlightened. I watched the video two more times, the third time sitting in meditation as he spoke, letting his wisdom wash over and inform me cellularly.

That's when Matrina popped in, as she tended to do. She stood before me smiling, wearing about every shade of sparkly pink imaginable. This was taking the "Glenda the Good Witch" thing a little too far. "Well, what did you think?"

"I loved that last one. Thank you so much for sharing it with me. He was amazing."

"And the others?" Matrina asked with a devious twinkle in her eye.

I didn't want to offend her, and frankly, I was still beating myself up over being so judgmental about the first two speakers. "Um, they were okay."

"No they weren't! They were crap!"

I was shocked! And then relieved. I laughed out loud, and Matrina joined me.

"You're learning the difference between discernment and judgment, honey. It's critical as you become more and more sensitive to the energy behind words. Don't beat yourself up for your clear perception."

"But I don't want to fall into the trap of being right again and making someone else wrong."

"Laudable, but misguided. It isn't that any one of those speakers was wrong. What you perceived was beyond right and wrong. Maybe for someone else, what they said would have touched home. For you, they didn't."

"But shouldn't I be able to find value in everything? Shouldn't I be able to listen to everyone and be patient enough to understand them?"

"Well, okay, and I suppose you should be able to withstand the pain of sleeping on a bed of nails. What's your point?"

"I feel guilty! Why do I feel guilty?"

"Let me see if I can clarify some things for you. A message was conveyed through each of those channels, meaning the speakers. You had a physiological response to each one, right?"

I thought back. She was right.

"Your body knew that falsehood existed—for you. Your discernment system was operational, so to speak."

"Operational? I feel like it went haywire. I felt like I had to vehemently protect myself from what they were saying. I have to admit I didn't even watch the first two videos all the way through."

"Good! And yes, you were protecting yourself. You were protecting yourself from a form of pollution, and your response was completely appropriate. We all need to learn the value of limiting our exposure to such assaults."

"But I thought that woman was stupid. I mean, isn't *stupid* a judgmental word?"

"Not if something really is stupid. There was a factual level of stupidity to that woman's speech. She had no experience about what she was saying. That doesn't mean *she's* stupid."

I started to feel stupid myself, as well as very tired...as I often do after speaking with Matrina. It's as if the logical side of my brain starts to disintegrate. I just wanted to lie down. But there was no stopping Matrina once she was in the flow.

"You thought the second speaker—the guy—was an egomaniac, yes?"

By this time I was pretty much over the fact that Matrina knew everything I was thinking...or had thought. "Yes."

"There's a certain truth to that. His speech was definitely directed by his ego and his need to steer the thoughts of others toward his way of thinking."

"Let me see if I understand what you're trying to tell me. You're saying that my initial impulse was right on and that there's an element of truth to what I'm calling my judgments? In other words, I didn't do anything wrong?"

"If you had used those judgments to feel superior or if you had taken them as fact, then I would have said that you went too far. But you had awareness the whole time. If anything, you were too hard on *yourself*, not on them."

"Wow, I don't think this is something that gets taught that often. I mean, I've never heard anyone say it's okay to be judgmental."

"No, honey, what I'm saying is that you *weren't* judgmental; you were discerning. You were asking yourself the right questions: *Why do I feel like this? Is it me? Is it them? What's going on?*"

"If I have a problem with something, isn't it always about me?"

"Yes and no. When I say to ask questions—is it me or them, for example—you are answering from within the frame of your perspective. Sometimes, it *is* them. You weren't feeling tired or angry or hungry or judgmental when you started watching, were you?"

"No. Actually, I was excited to get an email from you."

"So you weren't in full-blown reaction or steeped in your issues prior? You weren't 'having a bad day?'"

"No."

"Then doesn't it make sense that it had nothing to do with you, per se? Yes, it was your response, but it was your response to *them*—to their skilled or unskilled ability to transmit truth. You don't have to swim in a pool full of shit just to prove you're not judgmental of shit."

That one earned Matrina my double take. "The last video, though, that guy seemed to point right at the truth with every word he spoke. How did he do that?"

"That, my dear, was a master. He has experienced it, so he can talk about it."

"What a gift!"

"Thankfully, you had the ears to hear the message. Not everyone can hear through both ears into the heart." She suddenly sat up straight.

"That reminds me of a story!" Matrina said excitedly. "Once I was walking through a burial ground with the Sufi mystic Bayazid. He was one of my students, just as you are now. I needed to get him to stop wasting time and energy sharing his message with the wrong crowd. As we stepped over bodies, he noticed—perhaps with a little help from me—that in one corpse, there was a passage from one ear to the other. Yet on two other bodies we came across, there was no such passage or connection. He was quite perplexed and asked me about it, but as you know, I love building anticipation and just kept walking. Finally, we came across the body of a young woman. Her ears were not connected to each other, but a clear passage ran from each ear to her heart."

"So, why *were* the bodies so different?"

"There are three types of listeners in this world. The first group only hears through one ear, and that's as far as the message gets. The sound rattles about in their empty heads a bit and then—poof! It disappears. Others hear with both ears, but alas, it goes right through one ear and out the other. There are but a few rare souls, like the young woman, who take what they hear through the ears into their hearts. With such beings, the message lands and takes root."

"Mmm...I like that story."

"So you must always consider when sharing a message, 'Am I wasting my breath?'"

"I certainly hope you don't think that, Matrina!"

"I wouldn't be here if I did."

℘ ℭ

That weekend, a friend of mine invited me to a voice workshop, so I went hoping I might learn something new. Despite my initial excitement, I was really quite bored throughout the whole thing and kept wishing I were somewhere...anywhere...else. The facilitator was good at what she did, I suppose, but nothing she shared resonated with me. The group seemed to be enjoying themselves, but for some reason, I got more and more irritable. I finally reached the point where I couldn't stand one more second. I had to get out of there before I exploded! I needed to dance! I needed some funk music to shake my brain!

I got up my courage, grabbed my stuff, bid my friend goodbye, and left. I couldn't believe my luck...I got to the car just in time to avoid additional parking charges. Then my heart sank to my knees. I realized I'd left my keys back at the workshop. I'd have to go back for them...with my tail tucked between my legs. To make matters worse, the damn door to the building was locked! I *couldn't* get back in.

I had to wait for the workshop to end and someone to finally leave after all the long goodbyes and lingering thank yous. I spent another 20 minutes pacing by the door, dripping with anger. Instead of escaping a bad situation cleanly, with style and grace, I had to waste time waiting outside like a total idiot, I had to pay more for parking, and I didn't get home until much later, by which time I *had* exploded.

Matrina, with her impeccable sense of bad timing, was waiting for me, looking bright-eyed and irritatingly happy.

"Who would you be without your judgments, anger, and irritation?"

"I don't know," I answered with a slightly raised voice. I was in no mood for her games.

"Did you ever stop to think that maybe when you get this way, it's because you're tired or overloaded?"

"Yes, I realize that. But I still feel so ugly when I overreact. I get all hateful and stupid."

"Honey, when that happens, when you think you're ugly, play a beautiful piece of music and remember yourself." She crossed to my music collection, chose something, and put it on. The melancholy beauty of Beethoven filled the room, and we both just sat listening.

After twenty minutes, my mood shifted. Something inside me finally released. I was so grateful to Matrina for allowing me the space to work through everything. She didn't judge me or treat me like I had the Plague. She completely accepted me, and that made it somehow easier for me to accept myself.

"Did you know that you are music experiencing itself?"

"I've heard people say they have music in them, but I've never heard anyone say they *are* the music."

"We think music is limited and definable, a series of notes strung together and expressed through an instrument. Well, that last part is true, but almost *everything* is made up of notes and instruments. Our words are notes and our vocal chords are instruments. A dance is made up of notes played by the body. The breeze, a babbling brook, even the words on a page are all melodies. Everything is musical. All of Life is Music. You are music. Instruments merely try to replicate you. Drums, for instance, celebrate the heart. Strings are the sinew, the muscles, and connective tissues. The spinal column is akin to the piano.

And the wind instruments? They are the reeds of your arms and legs moving you forward. Can you guess what your voice is?"

I reviewed what she'd just said, "Heart, muscles, bones...I'm not sure. The skin?"

"Well, that's true in many respects, but I was shooting for Spirit. The voice is ether."

"Wait, ether? That's an element. Are each of the other instruments related to elements too? Because you only talked about corresponding body parts."

"Excellent question. Earth: drums. Fire: bones or piano. Water: strings. Air: wind instruments. Tada."

"Oh my God. That is so cool!"

"The mind does not create music, it recreates it. Music is a direct experience of the uncreated. We think we're the ones writing the songs that make the whole world sing. No, the whole world sings because it is song and longs to recreate and experience itself."

My mood had completed its one-eighty with her poetry. "Ah, Matrina. Thank you so much."

ౠ ౧౩

Over the next few weeks, Matrina introduced me to many new kinds of music. She said that music was my true teacher and that by listening, I would be better informed and forever changed by what I heard.

Most people understand the power of music to varying degrees. We seek its companionship in our automobiles, we plug into our devices and zone out, and we spend millions of dollars on vinyl, CDs, MP3s, concerts, and stereo equipment. Music plays in elevators, grocery stores, and over our phones when we're on hold. It takes on as big a role in movies as the actors. It's everywhere. Music has been a wonderful entertainment and release for us all. For many of us, it's also helped us turn within and deepen our understanding of ourselves.

"Today's lesson," Matrina said as she drove through traffic, "is to help you turn within and deepen your understanding of yourself."

"Where are we going?" She'd persuaded me to go on another mysterious adventure in her convertible, but this time the top was up so we could talk.

"Child," she tutted, "do you always need to know your destination?" She shook her head, then continued, somehow managing not to answer my question. "Music is a vehicle, just like a car or airplane, except the vehicle of music travels around, through, and within dimensions where cars and planes are simply too dense to travel."

"Listening to music definitely helps me escape."

"I'm talking about something much more important than escape. Get inside the music, become the music, and you can journey here, there, and everywhere in a flash, all at once. Because of music's ability to dance as it does—so free of earthly limits—and because of its ability to carry us, music is the key to a doorway you are only just now discovering. Music is the portal to the next world—one we create with our every thought, belief, and dream, with every word we speak and action we take."

"You make it sound so incredible. Music can do all that?"

The red light we were approaching turned green.

"And more! We know it soothes the savage beast. It really does carry the potential to heal our limited perceptions. For one thing, music is free of semantic constrictions. We listen and the mind is freed—not funneled into dense symbols and concepts."

"I don't know what I would do without it, myself. I know I need music just as much as I need air and food and water."

"It's that basic. Yet it's so much more. When we embrace the healing potential within music, we discover our potential for doing amazing things. These things won't come just to a select few, but to everyone willing to open his mind to strange and unfamiliar concepts. Music, sweet music, will carry us into the next world."

"Okay, music is everywhere, sure. Music can heal. I believe that. But I haven't heard of any Star Trek-like teleportations going on through music. Not even at a Phish concert. If you say it can happen, though, I'd like to believe it. How does it work?"

"You have to take your experience with music to the next level. You have to begin to work with music consciously as a tool for awakening your unlimited potential."

"And just how do you do *that*?"

"This application for music is just now being birthed—or should I say rebirthed? Music hasn't been used as intentionally as it can be, once was, and will be used again for such explorations."

We seemed to be hitting all the green lights. It was rather unusual and made me suspect Matrina had a hand in it.

She continued. "It's up to today's talented and conscious musicians to create music with pure intent—music that distills the very essence of life and opens doors to new experiences within it. I want you to join those of us called to build a new flying machine with wings of sound. If we start now, we're sure to arrive on time—without our baggage!" She giggled at herself.

"It sounds like you're talking science fiction."

"It's *all* fiction, remember? Here, let's listen to this." Matrina pulled out a CD and popped it into the player. The car filled with some very unusual sounds.

"What *is* this?"

"This is cyber-shamanic music created by Shapeshifter. It's electronica brought to life from the contributions of many realms and dimensions." The result was a multilayered audio experience beyond description. It was melodic in some places, dissonant in others, fast-moving, lulling, and then punching.

"This music has an intelligence that knows how to work with the human DNA, RNA, and other levels of matter and mind for healing and transformation."

"Matrina, this is all way out there. What are you talking about?"

"You really need to experience it. Guess we're going to have to see them in concert!" She pulled out a couple of tickets from her pocket.

So that's where we were headed.

℘℃℞

The Shapeshifter concert wasn't so much a performance as it was an experience...using sound, light, and movement shamanically...to shift and move energy on various levels, helping the participants in whatever healing they had to do.

We entered a hall...just a big open floor with no chairs. We were told to make ourselves comfortable. Fortunately, Matrina had brought along a couple of sleeping bags and pillows from in her trunk. This was going to be unlike any concert I'd ever been to.

A member of Shapeshifter began the introduction. "Historically, shamans—the spiritual leaders in tribal communities—have gone into other worlds to help people heal. Shapeshifter creates a space for an entire group to journey into the shamanic realm together, where they can intentionally create a new world. Those sensitive to energy can feel the energy in the room, play with it, and consciously help create and change it."

Someone in the audience raised a hand, "I've never been able to feel energy or see it."

"Those that can't feel it certainly can hear it and still benefit from it on a much deeper level than average perceptions allow. You may just come away with a newfound awareness of energy and intuitive ability. Up to now, our experience with music has been limited to the roles of creator and observer. We watch, and sometimes sing along, as the entertainer performs, or we play an instrument and hear our own creation, but we limit our relationship to what's happening. We ignore the *secret* realm and the healing powers of music."

"Secret realm?" someone asked, on behalf of many of us I'm sure, since I wondered the same thing.

"The true nature of music remains hidden and seemingly separate from us. But there are other experiences available outside of our misguided perception and belief that we're separate from the music. Shapeshifter invites you now to *become* the music."

It would be impossible to describe the journey I took at the concert. The music was so mysterious, so provocative. Healers worked the room offering energy work to one participant, then the next, adding another layer of vocal tones and sounds as they did so, while we let go into the music. Every now and then, someone would be inspired to get up and dance or even chant spontaneously with the music. There were percussion instruments at our disposal too.

As I listened, parts of the music carried me like a leaf floating on a river. I don't know if I just imagined all the things I saw, but I'd certainly never imagined anything like them before. First I was in deep space, floating among a galaxy of ringed planets, and then I was in a crystal world where everything was made of amethyst, quartz, sapphires, and emeralds. I landed in a wide-open field with grass the color of indigo, swaying under a bright orange sun, and then suddenly, I was surrounded by velvety black. It was here that I aligned with something that felt very powerful. It was the place from which all things spring in and out of existence. I can barely describe it. It was so beautifully empty and serene…a substance or non-substance like a blanket of black…so empty but so full. Pure magic.

I could also see with eyes open, not closed, the tendrils of music coming out of the speakers, rising up and spreading out across the room. I don't usually "see" energy and was astounded and touched by the music's beauty.

Matrina explained later that each concert Shapeshifter gives depends on the energies of all those present, as well as on the interactions that occur between the multidimensional perceptions and experiences available throughout the universe. Thus the music created is spontaneous, a different improvisation each time. The result is what can only be described as a living thing…music with an inexplicable intelligence and ability to transform the listeners into a greater state of presence and fluidity. The music is the bridge. It reveals to us that we are actually capable of existing in many dimensions at the same time.

I wasn't entirely sure I understood the word "multidimensional," so Matrina explained that the first dimension is comprised of atoms, molecules, and minerals. From there, we move into the realm of plants, trees, and animals. Then we enter into the human realm. Beyond that, there's the astral plane, the Heaven template, the Akashic records, and on and on, deeper and deeper into the unknown. I guessed that the velvety black place I'd experienced was pretty high up on the dimensional charts.

Working with Shapeshifter's music had a profound effect on my ability to listen. Because it wasn't music as I knew it, it pushed me to appreciate the unfamiliar and to find resonance with that. It definitely made it easier for me to find harmony within dissonance and to trust that dissonance also has its place. I could use the soundscapes in so many ways: to enhance my creativity while I wrote, to explore past the known boundaries of my imagination when I meditated, even to help me focus when I was studying something new. In that way, the soundscapes became soundtracks to the movie of my life.

PART III

BEYOND WORDS

Centuries ago, someone carved a phrase
over a doorway to a temple
The wisdom is so simple, powerful and true
but if you think you know the meaning, then it might not be
helping you

It doesn't mean you know your weaknesses
It doesn't mean you know your preferences
It doesn't mean you know your limitations
or the disappointments of your station

It doesn't mean you know your history
Your favorite color or your genealogy
The color of your hair and skin
or even much about the clothes you're in
It means so much more than everything you think inside that
head of yours

Know Thyself
There's greatness in you
Know Thyself
Your immensity, mystery, and majesty
Know Thyself
As part of everything and everyone
Know Thyself as Love

You see, if you know that you are quite divine
You'll never shoot another man from behind
And the only arms you'll care to bear
are the ones that hug and dare to share
To express yourself to all you see
To live in peace, and love, and harmony

for to Know Thyself I say to you true
is the freedom you seek to be absolutely you

The 7th Gate: Good Vibrations

I was finally on vacation, enjoying the sun and surf with a walk along the beach thinking, "Ah, no lessons, no challenges, no work, no problem!" I always felt so grounded, so connected by the sand and water. All those negative ions or something. A little time to myself would really help me integrate everything I had been learning. I stood and faced the water, a big smile on my face, breathing deeply when I sensed someone step up beside me.

"What a great place to learn what it means to be of sound mind and body, to become attentive, and to engage with sound as a transformational path."

"Matrina! What are you doing here?" She was wearing a yellow and green sundress and was barefoot. She was obviously enjoying the sand between her toes; I could see her digging and wiggling them in deep.

"What? Aren't you happy to see me?" she asked teasingly.

In that second, I remembered a dream I'd had the night before. It all came rushing back. "Matrina, I had the most amazing dream last night."

"Do tell!"

"I was listening to an old phonograph with a friend when this strange being came into the room and removed the needle from the record. I was like, 'Hey!' But he explained that what we were about to hear would have driven us crazy. He said it was the *Nada*."

"The *Nada*—yes, the All Sound. There are four dimensions of sound. The *Vaikhari* or course sounds we hear with our ears. *Madhyama* or mental sounds—the voices in our heads. *Pashyanti* or dream sounds. And then *Para* or transcendent sounds beyond the senses."

"My friend disappeared from the dream, but I wanted to

know what the *Nada* sounded like. 'Are you certain?' the being cautioned. 'Yes!' I told him. So he held a crystal up to my ear. I heard the most incredible buzzing…everything at once, all over the world. It just kept growing and growing in intensity until I woke up. Good thing I did because I really felt on the verge of exploding."

"What a treasure of a dream! *Pashyanti* moving into *Para*. Vibration is the source of all that is. It's the nature of creation. Sounds like your dream was a bit of a reverse-trace back to Source."

"I definitely feel changed by that dream. I feel quite insignificant."

"Humans are just little cells in the much larger system of Humanity and even smaller units in the system of the Earth. If we can learn to see across time and space past our limited, known existence, we can experience other parts of ourselves for the first time. We can begin to communicate with all that is, enhancing not only our own awareness, but making it easier for others to awaken as well. In fact, let's do a little meditation."

We plopped down onto the warm sand.

"Imagine for a moment the cells that comprise your body. Use your mind's eye to see those cells of your many bones, organs, muscles, and blood. Each cell has its own vibration, its own unique signature. Each system has its own collective vibration as well—the circulatory system, digestive system, respiratory system, nervous system, reproductive system, all of it. As everything within you vibrates, a symphony of sound is created."

I could almost hear it in that moment, like an orchestra warming up before a performance as they come into harmony.

"Now imagine that one little cell in your finger suddenly becomes aware. It recognizes itself, it hears the music created by all the other nearby tissues, and then, in a miraculous moment, it sees a heart cell across the gap beyond space and time. When it sees that little heart cell, it's in awe and in love. It listens to the rhythm of the heart cell, enraptured. It's still doing its little finger cell job, but now it knows that there is more to life than it realized.

"Now imagine that the little heart cell feels the love, the simple witnessing, coming from the finger cell and that the love is enough to awaken it. Then, across the great divide of time and space, the heart cell witnesses the finger cell. They see each other in a moment—across a crowded body full of cells just doing their jobs."

I laughed at that.

"They don't know each others' language, but they begin to play with one another. The finger cell vibrates *ta da* and the heart cell answers *ba dump*, slowly building a conversation. As this communication becomes more musical, more and more cells begin to awaken within this same body. Cells in the toes are making beautiful music with cells in the liver. The cells in the kidneys compose a delightful melody with cells in the lungs and blood. Soon, the body is an orchestration of awareness and aliveness. There is a communication happening, an exchange, an honoring. What does that feel like?"

"Exciting! Energizing! Joyful!"

After a moment, Matrina continued. "That's what toning is all about: an opportunity to communicate across time, space, and left-brain knowing. It's our chance to send out musical messages—vibrational greetings—to the many, many parts of ourselves we're only partly aware of, if we're aware of them at all. If we aren't aware, toning will make us so. When we tone, we learn to listen, to pay attention. We learn to contribute uniquely, with awareness, to the greater whole. This is a communication beyond words and languages and the division they create. It's universal."

"Matrina, you keep talking about toning! When are you going to teach me to do it?"

"Patience! First, it's important for you to understand some

things about sound as a healer."

"Like what?"

"To answer that, we go back to where we started—everything is vibration. We can't see radio waves, but we can tune into them and listen. We can't see microwaves, but they can cook our food—well, actually, they ruin our food, but that's another story. We can't see love, but we can definitely feel it."

"Okay, I understand that."

Matrina motioned out to the sea. "Our bodies are sound-sensitive instruments comprised of nearly 80% water. Water is a conductor of sound."

"What does that mean?"

"It means that sound affects our health! Think about the rhythm of the heart. When it's unsteady or racing too fast, something isn't right. For this beach towel to be a beach towel, its matter vibrates slowly, whereas the thoughts in your head are moving much quicker. Love is quicker still."

"Our health depends upon how we vibrate?"

"To put it simply. To fully understand how sound healing works, it's important to discuss two scientific terms: resonance and entrainment. Resonance is the frequency—or number of vibrations per second—at which an object naturally vibrates. Strike a tuning fork tuned to the key of G, and it resonates accordingly: in the key of G, not in the key of C or E. Resonance is natural. Like resonates with like."

"I get that. I say things like 'I resonate with that' all the time."

"Meaning you're aligned with it, in tune or in agreement with what's being said. As an example of resonance, imagine that you live on a busy street and that a very large truck speeds by. When it passes, objects on your shelves rattle slightly. Those objects are resonating. Can you think of another example of resonance?"

"Maybe when a picture falls from the wall when I slam a door? Not that I go around slamming doors or anything."

"Glad to hear it." She paused. "In terms of sound healing, we are usually working to raise our frequency."

"How?"

"Well, our second term will answer that question. Entrainment is the interaction between two closely related rhythmic cycles. We've talked about it before."

"Right, the tapping the foot thing. I only sort of understood that. Can you give me another example?"

"Rhythmic cycles have a mutual influence on one another. The stronger force always overcomes the weaker one. The most common example of entrainment involves a man named Christian Huygens."

"U-gens?"

She nodded. "Huygens observed the relationship between two pendulum clocks that had come into the same swinging rhythm. When two things are out of phase, such as two pendulums set into motion at different times, small amounts of energy are transferred that set up a negative feedback loop until they come into phase. The pendulums can move in completely different rhythms, but given time, they will either move into moments of synchrony, antiphase, or harmonic entrainment. In any case, the period of swing will be the exact same whether or not the phase is."

"Synchro-antipasto what? You lost me."

"I'll explain. Think of two people with opposing views trying to have a conversation. If one can persuade the other he's right, both individuals move into synchrony. If they discuss the issue to such extremes that they move into exact polar opposites of one another, then they are in complimentary entrainment — antiphase — or in your case, antipasto." She gave me a humoring look, her eyes peering over the rim of her sunglasses. "If they move into a complex and creative dance, seeing each other's point of view, then they're in harmonic entrainment."

"This is heady stuff. I think I'm starting to get it."

"Here's another example. It's common for women living

together in dorms or other close quarters to begin to menstruate with the same cycle. This is another example of entrainment. Similarly, think about how breathing slowly and steadily can bring a racing heart back to pace. Can you think of an example of entrainment?"

I tried.

"Pay attention to your environment."

"The waves! I am entraining to the waves. That's why I feel so relaxed here."

"It's certainly one of the reasons. While we're on the topic of waves, maybe I should mention that referring to sound as waves is a misnomer. They're actually *bubbles*."

"Bubbles?"

"Sound doesn't move in waves like scientists have always told us. It forms in bubbles. It's one of the reasons mantras are so powerful, but there I go again, getting ahead of myself."

We both tuned into the ebb and flow of the waves, forgetting everything for a moment. I must have fallen asleep; when I woke up, I was alone.

ဆ ၶ

Later, when I got back to the vacation condo, Matrina was sitting in front of the computer. She called me over.

"Enjoy your nap?"

"Yes, thank you." I'd never felt so refreshed!

"We've covered some pretty amazing stuff today. It's important to rest. It helps you integrate everything you've learned. Now then, Cymatics is the study of sound forms."

"I guess naptime is over," I said just in case the irony of her interrupting my vacation in the first place was lost on her.

"With its roots in the acoustical work of Ernst Chladni, Cymatics was developed by Hans Jenny, a scientist who tested the interactions of quartz sand with sine waves."

"Sine waves?"

"Simple tones."

"Don't you mean sine bubbles?" I asked. I wanted to show I'd been paying attention.

Not one to be distracted by semantics, Matrina ignored me, pulling up an online video to demonstrate a sine wave. A rather irritating sound came from the speakers.

"By placing sand on a vibrating plate or tonoscope," she said, "complex and beautiful geometric patterns emerge."

Sure enough, I watched as the sand began to shake around on top of a metal plate and form into geometric shapes.

"Jenny's science visually verifies that sound is what creates matter. We are no different than the sand on that plate. We too are 'sung into being' if you will."

"Wow! That is so cool."

We watched a few other videos to see more examples. With each varying tone, the resulting shape was different. From video to video, however, the same tone reproduced the same design again and again. It was fascinating.

"So now let's go back to entrainment. We're going to do a little visualization. Let's get comfortable." Matrina moved to the couch and I followed. "Close your eyes. Imagine yourself riding the train of your life—see yourself from the day you were born to the present moment, speeding from place to place, rushing to get things done. It all passes in a blur. Sensations, tastes, images, and feelings rush by."

I was catapulted into a life review as she spoke. I saw myself come into the world and experience play, school, romance, and work. I saw the faces of family, friends, teachers, and others who influenced me as I grew up.

"You wonder where the engineer is or if there even is one! At times, the train slows, but it never, ever stops. Even when it does slow down, it's never for long before it speeds back up again—faster now—as bits of info about your life and relationships and memories and other snippets pass without time to really see them—trends, news, fears, ideas, 'have tos', 'shoulds'."

It was dizzying, so much coming at me all at once. I began to feel as if everything was pulling at me, draining me of energy.

"Then suddenly, you hear a very clear bell, a tone that stops everything in time. The train freezes. Time stands still. All those rushing images stop."

I was suspended in time.

"Then you're drawn to that resounding tone of the bell, for you are beyond it all now. Thoughts begin to drift like clouds in a hot blue sky. Space expands. Even the space between the cells of your body seems to inhale and expand. Breathe and enjoy the breathing."

I'm not sure how much time had passed when I heard Matrina ask, "How do you feel?"

"Relaxed. Grateful to have stopped running around."

"So tell me what *you* think entrainment has to do with sound healing."

I thought about that for a moment and then said, "In every moment of our lives, we're entraining to one thing or another. It never stops unless we practice being in awareness. If the stronger force always entrains the weaker one, then it's up to us to be the stronger force in our own lives."

Matrina beamed at me. "As we resonate with the higher frequencies of love, compassion, and equanimity, we learn to radiate these qualities and not absorb everything that crosses our path. Perhaps more importantly, we have to be able to 'stop and wait' in order to choose what we entrain to in our day-to-day lives. In terms of offering our services to others, we need to be the stronger force, entraining everyone we meet to better health and well-being."

"Is that why I always feel so much better when you're around?"

"Perhaps. I hold my energy very high, and I know you can feel that. But I don't want you to become dependent upon me to feel that way. It's in you too."

ॐ ௸

Right before bedtime that night, Matrina came to me once more, all bouncy and bright. I don't know where she got her energy. Didn't she ever get tired? She caught me in the middle of a bedtime snack.

"I hope I didn't overwhelm you earlier. We covered a lot today, and I know integrating all that information can be quite stressful."

"Me? Overwhelmed?" I laughed, feeling a little punchy. "What makes you say that?" I took another bite of the giant hot fudge sundae on my lap. "I always eat a half gallon of ice cream before bed…in bed…with Kermit here."

"Child, don't talk with your mouth full." Matrina left the room for a moment, and I could hear her opening and clanging shut the kitchen drawer. She came back with a spoon and dug in…uninvited, I might add. "I just want to give you a little more to think about as you enter the dreamtime."

I groaned.

"The body is really one big resonator—one big plate. The vagus nerve, the largest nerve in the body, runs from your ear through most of your body, including almost all of your internal organs. Through the medulla, the auditory nerve connects with all the muscles in the body. Your muscle tone, equilibrium, flexibility, and vision are all affected by sound. The vagus nerve connects your inner ear with your larynx, heart, lungs, stomach, liver, bladder, kidneys, small intestine, and large intestine. Your ears control your body's sense of balance and act as the conductor of your entire nervous system."

I was astounded. "I remember you saying that we listen with our whole bodies, not just with our ears. Is this what you meant?

I had no idea."

"There's more. The ear is made to pick up a wide range of high frequency sounds, but as we've discussed, most of what we hear day to day is low frequency—traffic, machines, computers, lights, appliances, and so forth. High frequency sounds, on the other hand, are what replenish the brain and activate the cortex. We need high frequency sounds. It's all about frequency!"

"I get the feeling you're talking about more than music."

"Of course. The question to ask yourself is: how high can you keep your frequency when you're faced with anger, fear, war, financial crisis, or any of the other million concerns that pop up daily?"

That laser-like look of intensity took over Matrina's eyes. I could tell she was about to go off on one of her profound tangents. I tried to concentrate, a sugar headache coming on.

"The science of Cymatics reveals how vibration creates form. It reveals our birth—for we, like the sand, are subject to vibration. Some unseen, unheard song is creating us—singing us into being. We are the sand upon the vibrating plate, taking shape into our existence, believing we are the peaks and points that take form, and believing we are this or that. In reality, we're malleable, moldable, and at the mercy of the Great Sound. For if this great sound were to cease or be disrupted, these mighty houses we've constructed would disperse like so many grains of sand flung to the wind.

"Something is conscious of us. It listens as it plays upon the instruments that we are. It takes delight in the cacophony, an orchestration so grand it is far beyond our contemplation. It is masterful, elegant, swift, and awesome. It is the Song of the Universe—and more. It is our Composer, and one who loves beyond conditions, beyond the beyond. If the law of 'as above, so below' holds true, then we too are composers. We too sing songs that breathe shape into reality. But are we listening? Are we paying attention to the compositions we create?

"What is our rhythm? What order are we singing out of the chaos? Are we in harmony with the Great Sound? Do we breed forgiveness or hatred with the words we speak? Do we give form to self-pity and blame or to maturity and wisdom? Do we relinquish our masterpiece to our reasoning minds, ignoring the awkward thud that deflates our spirit? Do we allow the voices of others to influence our melody with fear or with hope? What are the consequences to our choices? Someone is *always* listening. What are you saying?

"In essence, our words do not matter. They are but sand upon a plate. *You* are the vibration that stirs the sand. You are the energy that forms the peaks and points and geometric patterns. Where is your faith? In words? In meanings that were forced upon you? Or is your faith in your own musicianship? Can an artist infuse hatred with love, fear with love, resentment with love, violence with love? Yes! Reclaim the symbols and be Love, sing Love, create Love, perpetuate Love. Make sure the music that everyone hears in your presence is the Divine Song, no matter what."

"Thank you, Matrina. That's one hell of a bedtime story."

"Sweet dreams."

෨ ෬

Vacation over, weeks later, Matrina and I were browsing a local music store. There was no end to her fascination with all kinds of music.

"Quiz time, Wrenne! What can you tell me about sound as a healer?"

"Well, frequency can be used to entrain the body, emotions, mind, and spirit in ways that bring us balance."

"How would you know what frequency to apply?"

"Um...I don't have a clue," I said quite honestly.

"Many people involved in sound healing take a very scientific approach. They conduct studies and determine that a particular frequency resonates with a certain body part—that a certain interval has a particular effect. I prefer to operate from a more multidimensional and intuitive approach."

"What do you mean?"

"For me, it's more psychological. The scientist may say, 'This sound at such and such a hertz brings about a particular affect and should therefore be used only in such and such a way.' There is nothing wrong with that approach, but it isn't one I share. I'm more likely to say, 'When I listen to this in this moment, I feel this—although that may change in the next moment.'"

"So it's better to just see what feels right?"

"Don't get me wrong. I respect the science behind sound healing. Perhaps the best approach is one that blends a bit of science with intuition. When we consider that we only understand about 3% of our brains and that 3% is where science dwells—"

"Wait. I thought it was a myth that we only use 3% of our brains."

"I didn't say that we *use* 3%; I said we only *understand* 3%. It makes sense, therefore, that coming from science alone is limiting. Our intent or faith, combined with the vibration of sound, is really what creates healing and growth."

"So it's part science, part intuition, part intent." I was looking through the used music bin and came across an old Gospel music CD I used to own. "Oh my gosh, I used to listen to this every time I cleaned the house! It always helped me keep moving."

"Oo, good topic! Let me ask you: Would you ever relax to a military march?"

"Of course not. I'd listen to something slow and soothing."

"Ever listened to slow, meditative music in the car?"

"Er, I generally need something a little more lively when I'm driving or I get sleepy."

"There's a reason we listen to what we listen to. And whether we're listening to it by choice or exposed to it in our environment, music does affect us. It can slow us down, quicken our pace, wake us up, or soothe us emotionally. I want you to begin to pay attention to the effect music has on you in any given moment. When you're shopping, what's playing? Does it make you spend more money? That's likely because that's why they play music in stores."

"Actually, I walked out of a store the other day because the music felt assaulting. So I guess their plan doesn't always work."

"Was the music too loud?"

"Yes. There was no space to consider the clothes I wanted to buy."

"Interesting. Have you ever noticed when eating out if the restaurant played music to fit the atmosphere?"

"Actually, yes, I have noticed. Once, at a Chinese restaurant, they played this crazy rock and roll. It was incongruent…and incidentally gave me indigestion."

"The next time you're out to eat, notice if there's too much noise going on at once in your environment—TVs on one end, piped-in music on the other, and dinner conversation in between. I have yet to understand why we do this to ourselves. Also, when you watch a movie, notice what kind of background music is playing. Does the music evoke emotions that fit the story?"

"I remember a teacher demonstrating this to our class in high school. He showed part of a scary movie with no sound. It seemed ridiculous, but then with the sound turned up, the music made us all edgy and spooked."

"It isn't just music, though. All sound has an impact on us— all the time. We can close our eyes, but we can't really close our ears; they're always vulnerable to outside influence. In fact, the stapedius muscle that regulates a tiny middle ear bone is always at work. It never takes a break."

"Really? Wow! Even the heart takes a break after every beat.

So if every sound has an impact on our being, what's the difference between noise and music?"

"Excellent question. For our purposes, let's think of noise as negative, in that it depletes our energy with disorder, chaos, and fragmentation. Noise is destructive. Music, on the other hand, gives us energy. It is ordered, coherent, and whole. I'm using a very broad meaning of music here, just as there is music in birdsong or the crashing of waves. While noise adds to our stress and fatigue, music relieves it."

"I remember when I used to teach elementary school that Mozart's music was thought to help children learn. Now, some experts have proclaimed that listening to music can treat autism, attention deficit disorder, and even dyslexia. So I'm not surprised at all to hear you say that music has a positive effect."

"It's not always positive, though. I'm sure you've heard about experiments in which plants are exposed to different kinds of music to see how they respond. Harsh music has been shown to affect plants negatively. They grow to be more feeble, malformed, and sickly than their counterparts exposed to gentler music—like classical."

"But I like rock and roll. Are you telling me it's bad for me?"

"Maybe. Maybe not. We have a different intelligence than plants. Perhaps our mental preferences inoculate us. The point is that chaotic sounds have chaotic impacts on matter. Chaos isn't good or bad, but it is still chaos. Too much of it can throw us out of whack."

"Don't we have some power over the negative effects?"

"Perhaps, but not much. Noise stimulates us. It shakes up our composition and can throw us out of balance. What happens when we get off balance?"

"We don't feel so great?"

"Right, our health deteriorates. All kinds of illnesses can be attributed to noise. It impacts our nervous system, disrupts our sleep, and can wreak havoc on our cardiovascular system, emotional state, even our hormones. With overexposure to noise, we become as sickly as those plants I mentioned. There's a reason that the government blared all-night music and irritating noise during the Branch Davidian crisis in Waco, Texas, back in the 90s."

"I remember that. There was some kind of armed cult holed up in a compound, so law enforcement tried to drive them out with constant noise."

"It drove them crazy. You would be amazed at the correlation between the use of sedatives and psychotropic prescription medicines and the amount of noise pollution in the environment."

"You mean, there's a higher use of such drugs when noise is ever-present?"

"Exactly. It's critical to become more and more aware of how sounds in your environment affect you on a daily basis. Only through awareness can we make changes that benefit ourselves and others."

The 8th Gate: Toning

The sun was setting as I walked along a riverbank close to home, noticing that the trees looked like chalk drawings and that the bluebirds gracing the purple and orange-tinted skies created a sharp contrast. There were people on either side of the sapphire river: a group having a picnic, others talking, even a father and son flying a kite. Filled with joy, I began to hum, feeling lighter and lighter until my feet began to lift off of the ground and...

"Wake up, Wrenne. Today's the day you've been waiting for."

I thought I might still be sleeping. "Finally!" I said rolling over to see Matrina, dressed in white, standing at the side of my bed. For a second, I mistook her for an angel. "Wait," I asked, snapping awake, my delightful dream now a fading memory. "What have I been waiting for?"

"Today, you'll learn about vocal toning."

"Finally!" I said, happy my initial response had been accurate.

"Toning is an opportunity to communicate across time and dimensions. It transcends left-brain knowing. It's our chance to send out musical messages—vibrational programming—to the many, many parts of ourselves. When we tone, we learn to really listen—to *pay* attention without breaking the bank, so to speak. Toning is about managing our attention. We learn to contribute our unique expression, with awareness, to the greater whole. As I mentioned before, it's communication beyond words and languages and the divisions they create. Toning is universal. Would you be surprised if I told you you've been toning since you were born?"

"Well, yes. *Have* I been toning since I was born?"

"Actually, you were born toning. You entered this world with a tone."

"You mean my first cry?"

"Yes, and the idea of toning is as old as the human ability to make sound. Cultures the world over have practiced some form of toning, whether consciously or not."

"So if we've all been doing it since we were born, why do we need to learn to do it now?"

"We take it for granted that we are sound-makers because it comes so naturally. We cry out, we yelp, we whimper, we laugh. But we don't think about it much. That's the trouble. For one thing, as children, we quickly learn that certain things aren't allowed. In fact, we often stifle our cries, whether of joy or grief, so as not to disturb others. It's just not acceptable to appear emotional or excitable. As we've already seen, we use our words quite mindlessly, to insult and sabotage ourselves and others."

"Yes, that's unfortunately true."

"How about a little history lesson?"

"Sounds boring."

"Not this one."

Matrina put her hand over my eyes, and suddenly I was traveling in a dream with her through time and space. I could hear Matrina's voice narrating as I was lifted up over the Earth. In a flash, everything started to disintegrate...the Earth, the moon, the stars...back to the tiniest atom, until even that disappeared. Then the entire process reversed, and I was awestruck, witnessing the birth of everything.

"Within awareness—the great primordial expanse—sound was born. And with that sound, all manner of matter was made manifest."

I experienced the creation myth that has taken so many forms in so many languages since time began. First came the word. I could hear a great and complex orchestra stirring as specks of matter came together to form every geometric shape imaginable. It reminded me of the particles of sand on the tonoscope.

"Humans are musical creatures, born of sound. All ancient cultures and mystical groups have been aware of this. They all claimed, through different stories—the creation myths of

Hinduism, Sikhism, and Hermeticism, and of the Chinese, Egyptian, and African cultures—that the Universe began with a sound. The ancient mystery schools of Greece, China, India, and Tibet—among others—included teachings on the healing benefits of Sacred Sound. Certain tones among the Chinese and Tibetans, for example, are believed to hold unique power. Cultures the world over have ancient practices in healing tones and sacred mantras."

She removed her hand, and we were back in my living room. It took me a moment to fully come back into my body.

Matrina explained, "The fact that each culture traditionally reveres different tones reminds us that our intent is always at the heart of every matter. Toning is a natural phenomenon, a means of expression and creation. Our ancestors understood sound to be a bridge between the visible and invisible, and so they developed ways of working with that tool through meditation, prayer, and ritual. But we have been trained out of this natural form of expression through the process of our contemporary domestication."

"We're domesticated?"

"As children, we're wild and free with our voices. We 'vroom vroom' with our toys and sing made-up tunes to our dollies. We cry in public when we're upset—even scream sometimes—but someone is always there to tell us to be quiet, to shut up, or to wait until later when it's more appropriate. We quickly learn that our voice is something at best to be trained, tamed, and caged, or at worst, silenced altogether."

"I get it. Just like a dog is trained not to pee on the carpet, we are trained to be socially acceptable no matter how much it goes against our nature."

"Vocal toning is the means to restore balance to all of our systems, inner and outer. It is a way to access the deepest parts of ourselves and other realms that wish to guide and heal us. Let's do an important exercise now in feeling sound. To some extent, we've been doing this all along."

Matrina made a low *OM* tone. She then had me match the tone.

"How does the sound *OM* make you feel?"

"Grounded. Centered."

"Where do you feel it?"

I repeated the sound and took note. "In my legs, lips, face."

"What kind of impact does the sound have on you?"

"Well, it seems like more than just a feeling; I *feeeeel* myself resonate with it. The effect seems to grow, if that makes sense, like the ripple created from a stone thrown into a pond. I feel like I'm protected by concentric rings farther and farther out from myself."

"These are key questions I've asked. It's essential to pay attention, to be comfortable noticing whatever is happening. Only then can you modify the practices in a way that will be most beneficial to you. Only then can you use toning as a healing tool."

I nodded. It made sense.

"Toning teaches us how to become skillful listeners. When we tone intentionally, we direct our attention. We begin to hear what once was unnoticed."

"So it will develop my sense of hearing?"

"Hearing, feeling, knowing. One tone at a time."

ॐ ॐ

Before we got much further into toning, Matrina taught me several physical warm-ups to help prepare me for the practice of sounding.

"It might be helpful to think 'head down' in order to remember the sequence. Start with the jaw. Using your fingertips, feel for the little indentations between the upper and lower jaw about an inch in front of your ears. You'll know it when you feel it because one fingertip will fit nicely."

I slackened my jaw and gave it a little massage. The area was surprisingly tender and loved the attention.

"Now move the jaw very gently up and down and side to side. Don't overdo it. We're just getting a sense of your range of motion there."

My jaw felt very tight.

"Here, try this."

Matrina put a pencil between her teeth, with the incisors just over the top. Placing her elbows on the table, she held the ends of the pencil, dropping her lower jaw open, her hands keeping the pencil...and her head...in place.

"You try. That's right. Breathe and relax. Breathe and relax. Put your weight, the weight of your head, on the pencil allowing the jaw to just let go."

I felt my jaw begin to soften.

"Now let's revisit the tongue, shall we? We're better able to articulate when it's relaxed and flexible. Here we go. Oh, and this one can get messy!"

She had me stick out my tongue as if trying to touch my chin with it. Then I flexed my tongue up, as if trying to touch the tip of my nose. Next, I stretched my tongue from ear to ear. Then came the messy part. She told me to pretend my face was covered in whipped cream. She had me swipe my tongue over my upper lip and around, stretching it to get as much of the whipped cream as possible. I felt like Jabba the Hut in *Return of the Jedi*.

"Continue clockwise, from the side of your mouth to the bottom lip, up the other side and back to the top. Now reverse directions. If you aren't getting wet, you aren't doing it right."

"Oh, I'm getting wet all right. Gross!"

"Make contact with the skin. Great!"

I wiped my mouth.

"Now open your mouth and pop your eyes really wide. Try to look beyond surprised."

Matrina made a face, and I couldn't help but laugh.

"Go on, try it."

So I did, holding the stretch for a moment. Then she had me do the opposite…scrunch everything up, my mouth, eyes, and brow.

"Pinch. Pinch. And release. How does that feel?"

"Fine."

We continued with some neck rolls and shoulder shrugs to loosen those muscles.

"Okay, now for our final warm-up. Ever notice how an animal shakes off trauma or fright?"

I nodded, thinking about how a horse whinnies.

"This last exercise can help us remember to do the same. It's called the Chi Gong Shakes."

For this one, I had to stand up, feet about hip width apart. She had me spread my toes and grip the floor so I'd feel really grounded. Then I began to bounce my body with little pulses, as if I were standing on a trampoline. As I bounced, I felt my weight and center of gravity redistribute. I was then able to sink even further into each bounce.

"Bring everything into the bounce. You are holding your head rigid. Let it feel the pulse too."

The more I sunk into it, the better it felt…like everything was being shaken off and thrown into the ground. I did this for about a minute.

"Now shake off your hands like they're dripping with water. That's it. Let go. Okay, now stop. Stop and feel and breathe."

I felt incredibly warm, alive, relaxed, and ready to go.

"Now that we're warmed up, let's take a few minutes to talk about groaning and moaning."

"I promise I'll stop."

"Funny. But that's not what I mean. From my perspective, groaning and moaning are wonderful practices."

"I've had lots of practice."

"Focus! First of all, bring to mind times when you heard someone naturally moaning or groaning. I'm referring to the sounds made here, not the content of speech. When do people groan?"

"Usually, when they're in severe pain or discomfort. It could also be when they're experiencing pleasure too, I suppose."

"Yes, groaning is a release of pent up energies."

"What about moaning? Is that different?"

"Typically, we moan when pain or pleasure is more consistently present or drawn out. When we are in a weakened, vulnerable state, we moan—whether we're weakened by grief or by the world's most incredible piece of chocolate. There's a definite energetic difference between moaning and groaning. One of your tasks this week is to discover that difference for yourself."

"My homework is to groan and moan?"

"Groaning and moaning with intent, yes. We can help our bodies purge blockages of stale energy or emotions this way. You know, when we're young, we don't think twice about making these kinds of sounds. Remember domestication? When we grow older, we become socially conditioned to restrain ourselves from letting go with indelicate or attention-getting sounds. A completely natural and healthy process becomes inhibited by the mind. As a result, all the energy and emotion that's normally discharged gets stuck and jammed up in our systems. We're carrying years and years of this stuff around with us!"

"I totally get that. I remember years ago hitting my head very hard when my landlord happened to be in my apartment. I wanted to scream bloody murder and cry like a big baby, but I didn't because I was too embarrassed. I held it all in. The pain was excruciating for two days! I thought I'd have to go to a doctor if I didn't do something. I finally started allowing my body to make the sounds I'd held in. I immediately felt better. Of course, it still took me days to completely work out what I could've released instantly! Live and learn."

"Hmm. In that case, I think we should implement a little growling. You see, when we don't express our moaning and groaning, it compacts and can turn into anger. Here, stand up."

I did. Matrina stood directly in front of me and put up both her hands, palms out.

"Here. Push against my hands with your hands."

We leaned into each other, repelling each other's weight.

"Good. Now start growling and push against me."

It felt a little awkward, to say the least. I was afraid of being too forceful, but frankly, my growls were more like meows.

"Don't be a pussy. Come on, push. Growl! Find that animal power and let it out!"

I felt anger rising up from my belly. I pushed harder and Matrina matched me. I began a deep, low growl that gradually rose in volume. My face contorted; my eyes flashed. I felt alive and strong!

"That's it. Give it to me. Don't stop now."

I went on and on until I was sweating and exhausted.

"Great! Now relax. Sit down here. Don't speak. Just be."

I sat on the couch and closed my eyes. Within seconds, I began to cry. I couldn't stop. I was releasing years and years of God only knows what. Matrina didn't try to comfort me. She just stood by as a compassionate witness and let me be there for myself. Eventually, I calmed down. I blew my nose and realized my whole body was tingling. I felt great. Better than great. I felt huge!

Matrina had me experiment with the *ZZZ*, *GRRR*, *RRR*, and *VVVR* sounds for groaning. Then I made some moaning sounds using *MMM* and *NNN*. I felt myself bearing down, forcing myself to make the sounds at first, but eventually I was able to stop resisting and really let go. Then the sounds felt less contrived. They seemed to rise up with a life of their own.

Funny thing about this exercise. In time, I found myself being much more spontaneous with my voice. I sang out with the songs playing in the grocery store. When I stubbed my toe, I didn't stifle my response. Instead, without even thinking about it, I cursed and then toned. When I went out to eat with friends, I took great pleasure in moaning over my dessert!

ᎧᏋ

Once I was comfortable with moaning and groaning, Matrina introduced me to key elements of toning.

"Remember your alphabet?"

"You know I do."

"Here's where the fun really begins—the most basic of tools for toning. The smallest elemental units of language are the vowels—*A, E, I, O, U*—and consonants, as you know. The simplest forms of toning focus on the vowels. We'll get into the respective vowel sounds more deeply in a moment. Without vowels, consonants would be very difficult if not impossible to produce."

I had to try it. I tried making the sound *D* without a vowel. No matter how I tried, I couldn't say the letter without also saying *EE* or *UH* at the end. I tried it with *M*. I made the *MMM* sound and thought I had just performed a miracle until Matrina pointed out the name of the letter is *EM*. It can't be said without the *EH*.

"Once we add consonant sounds, we are toning syllables, which add a completely different feeling to our experience. The consonants *M* and *N* for instance, add a calming, nasal quality to our sounding. The consonants *H* and *K* tend to add explosive, solar plexus power. *R* and *Y* add a grounding element. There are also chants or mantras, and then actual melodies containing strings of lyrics. Each form of sounding has its place, its power, and its purpose. Remember, in all languages, there is a meaning for every letter and combination of letters that we call words.

"I got this! Words are channels of energy that we infuse with meaning."

"Yes. There are different levels of meaning, beginning with denotation—or the external meaning of words—"

"And the connotation, or the personal and associative meaning of words."

"There is also a secret or hidden meaning to words. It's said that when you understand the secret meaning of words, you have unlocked the mysteries of the universe."

I remembered Cymatics had shown that ancient Sanskrit syllables produce the same geometric shape again and again. In the case of *OM*, it was a shape used by the people of that time to graphically represent the sound. "I guess we are somewhat removed in the present day from the mystical powers of language."

"Indeed, we've lost touch. Vowels were often left out of many early alphabets and holy books. It was believed that the vowels contained a power that was dangerous if released carelessly. So while letters are just little figures on a white page, what they represent is extremely powerful. Letters began as sounds that were eventually transformed into written units, but the sounds are what carry the power. Try this." She handed me a book. "Look at a page without reading. Simply scan your eyes over the page. Notice anything?"

"I'm not sure what you mean. The words aren't reading themselves aloud or anything." As I looked at the page, it became very difficult not to recognize the symbols I knew so well. "I guess it takes my mind...my interpretation of the symbols...to bring the page to life."

"In effect, when you read, you are hearing the words in your head. In the most obvious way, it's this construction of meaning that gives words power, but it's important to realize that even without the meaning we impose upon words, the sounds themselves have power." She took the book back and put it down. "According to traditional toning methods, each of the vowels is associated with an energy center of the body."

"You mean chakras?"

"Yep. But don't get caught up in the idea that certain sounds are right and others wrong. This is all just a starting point; I want you to know that going in. So let's look more deeply at the vowel sounds, long and short. The long vowels say their names—*A-E-I-O-U*. The short vowels are more complicated, so we'll focus on the main ones—*AH* as in *amen*, *EH* as in *enter*, *IH* as in *intelligent*, *AW* as in *octave*, *OO* as in *pool*, and *UH* as in *understand*."

I knew these sounds already, of course, but Matrina helped me understand that there were many ways I could change each tone. I could play with volume and pitch, as well as where I placed the note physiologically and how long I held each tone. I could also vary the amount of breath I used, to control how forceful or soft I was with my onset.

"Man, there is so much more to this than I ever realized. I feel uncoordinated." I uttered a quiet *OO*.

"Don't be afraid to be loud. Play with how that feels too. In fact, let's work with volume for a moment. Using the sounds *AH HA*, begin by singing it very quietly."

I let out a whisper of an *AH HA*.

"Now gradually increase your volume, noticing with your full attention anything you feel emotionally or physically."

I followed her instructions and found that I wanted to modify the sound by prolonging the *AH* and shortening the *HA*, but I didn't think I was supposed to.

"Follow that impulse!"

Matrina must have noticed I was censoring myself. I modified the sound and gradually increased my volume, finally letting out a very loud and satisfying *AH HA*.

"What did you notice?"

"It felt great! It was almost a relief to take up so much space with my voice. I'm so glad you told me to follow my impulse."

"You just learned something very important. Your body

knows best. I can tell you what to do, but ultimately, you must listen and obey your inner voice. When an exercise begins to take you in an unexpected direction, honor it. If you don't, you'll never be able to deepen your practice. Which reminds me, I have something for you."

She dug through her bag and handed me a stack of books.

"Each of these books talks about toning through the chakras as a practice, and each one says it should be done in an entirely different way."

"That's confusing. Which one is right?"

"Toning is as unique as the individual expressing it. So there isn't one right way for everyone. It isn't about being right or wrong. So be curious. Have fun! If something doesn't feel good, alter it. It's about experimenting and honoring what's true for you. If you find yourself wondering, 'Am I doing this right?' — change the question. Tell yourself, 'That was interesting.' Then ask, 'Can I do this yet another way?'"

If I'd learned anything in my studies with Matrina, it was that there's no single correct method that's right all the time. The "best" method is the one that honors your intuition. The best application of any practice is the one you modify at the time to be most in harmony with your needs on all levels: physical, mental, emotional, and spiritual. I'm grateful to Matrina for helping me understand the value of personal discovery.

"When you tone, experiment with the shape of your lips, the position of your jaw, the placement of your tongue, and where you place the sound—be it in your chest, your nasal cavity, or a combination of the two. There are so many possibilities! The best way to become aware of them is by exploring. Okay, are you ready? Let's tone the sound *EE*."

I let ring a clear high *B* on an *EE*.

"There's something to be said for the female voice. It might not be able to impact matter the way the bass tones can, but it can increase frequency and raise us up in a way the male voice can't.

Did you know that while middle C vibrates at about 256 Hz per second, high C vibrates at 4096!"

"That's quite a difference."

"Do you know your lowest comfortable pitch?"

I wasn't quite sure how low I could go, so Matrina had me do a slide from a comfortable note down the scale until I could go no further. Then we did a siren-like exercise moving up and down the scale of my personal vocal range. She told me to pay attention as I did this exercise to places where the voice seemed to want to hang out. She said the siren is a technique used in sound healing to help target an appropriate tone for healing purposes.

Once I had the hang of this process, Matrina introduced me to something called Sanskrit seed syllables: *OM, SHAM, HAM, YAM, RAM, VAM,* and *LAM.* Each syllable was related to a different chakra or energy system of the glands. We sang them one at a time, then mixed and combined them into strings of melody, then strung them all together in one breath. I paid attention to how and where each one resonated within me. I noticed how certain combinations felt good to say, like a balm on my hurts or a boost of energy when I felt tired.

These sounds were powerful!

Matrina gave me a list of questions to ask myself while toning to build my awareness of its effect: "Does the tone feel 'right on' or does something feel off? Can you identify what that is? How can you modify the exercise so it feels right? Do you feel the sound not just in your physical body, but in your energetic body as well? Where and how? What qualities does the energy have? Is it balancing, exciting, energizing, calming, heating, cooling, or even draining? Do you feel more aligned and in harmony with life? Does that feeling last and if yes, for how long after you practice? Does any sensation change as you tone? Do you notice your body wanting to move or dance with a sound? Do you feel inhibited in any way? Are you resisting an exercise?"

These questions helped me really tune into my inner

guidance, strengthening my ability to perceive subtle shifts within. I started to see that there was a communication happening deep within me between the tones I made and the various parts of my body and that if I paid attention, I could "get the message." Over time, I could modify my tones in ways that felt more authentic, healing, and satisfying.

৯৩ ৫৩

Once I had a handle on the basics of toning, Matrina encouraged me to attend another special circle...in person this time. So I attended a group with about 15 people. I recognized some of the faces from the invisible visit I made with Matrina months ago and wondered whom among them she had also taught. I felt a little nervous, so I just listened at first, taking in the toning voices around me. A beautiful thunderstorm was rolling in, and it eventually inspired me to add my voice into the group mix.

Matrina had prepared me by explaining that her circles usually focus on Free-Form Toning, which lends itself to a wider variety of expression than Straight Toning. In Straight Toning, you stay on the same vowel tone and pitch for one full breath. In Free-Form Toning, you can dramatically change each tone, be it a single vowel or a combination of vowels or even a syllable, within a single breath. Sounding...the act of toning... can even include rhythm-making.

Directly to my left in the circle was a woman whose voice started to grate on my nerves. She was making these very strange sounds, loudly. Here I was trying to sing with beauty and reach some kind of harmonious relationship with everybody, and this darned woman wouldn't cooperate. I really struggled with my reaction.

I spoke to Matrina about it later as we sat outside. The rainstorm had swept through, and the sun had returned.

Matrina explained, "Toning in a group is probably one of the most powerful teaching environments. You not only learn to trust yourself, but to listen very deeply. Toning in groups can trigger all sorts of judgments towards yourself and others, giving you a wonderful opportunity to transform them."

"That woman, I guess she wasn't really listening very deeply."

"That may or may not be true. You're missing the point. It's never about the other person, no matter how much you want to make it so."

As if on cue, a beautiful rainbow appeared in the sky to the east. We both paused to enjoy its beauty.

"What is a rainbow?" Matrina asked.

"An optical illusion?"

"Isn't everything!" Matrina laughed. "It's white light separated into each of its components—red, orange, yellow, green, blue, and purple—each color with its own distinct frequency. We need all those colors to recombine into white light. If any one of those colors disappeared, we'd no longer have white light, nor would we have that beautiful rainbow. Something would be missing."

"Okay…where are you going with this?"

"When toning, the instant we discount another's voice, devalue one sound over another, or have any preference, we are making white light impossible and buying into the illusion of separation. By virtue of its definition, nothing can be excluded from wholeness. As you tone, forget what anyone else is doing— forget what *you* are doing if you can and just allow the alchemical process to take over. Try to let go of the mind and allow everything. How much beauty were you personally able to hear as you listened to what you were creating collectively?"

"I guess I was able to do that to some extent. But I definitely had a preference for the harmonious…the balanced."

"Most people do. It's natural, but not necessarily enlightened. We can't evolve *and* stay in our comfort zone. We need to move past the familiar, the known, and the learned to experience what lies beyond. When we can be with sounds, experiences, and stimulation that once made us uncomfortable and still feel equanimity, we are at peace. These sessions, this work, and sound itself are passages into the unknown. They challenge all those places within us where we contract, fear, judge, and separate. Sound is a healer with its own intelligence; it works in dimensions beyond our mental comprehension. When we let go of our need to know, we can come to peace through our acceptance of what is. That is the intent and practice of Toning for Peace."

Matrina encouraged me to start leading my own toning circle, saying it would help me go deeper and let go of some of my attachments with sounding. I was a little hesitant and unsure of myself. Had I even come close to mastering the skills? In the end, I let go of the idea that I needed to be perfect. I got a group of friends together to tone and soon realized that Matrina was right. I learned things by facilitating the group that I never would have learned otherwise.

ೞ ೧೩

After I'd been toning for some time, Matrina spoke with me about combining toning with meditative intent. She explained that at this level of toning, the practice took the practitioner much deeper into the mysteries of sound.

"Vocal toning without meditative intent is pretty much just entertainment with some physical, emotional, and mental benefits. With intent, vocal toning can increase your personal frequency, making it possible for you to stay for longer and longer periods in high energy. It also opens up a channel of communication with your higher self."

"My intention is to meditate then?"

"First, I'd like to make a clear distinction between the words *intent* and *intention*. Intention is just one of many possibilities. It's a bit wishy-washy. Intent is like a laser cutting through to the outcome you want. If you ever want to know what you are intending, just look around you. There it is! Intent is the launching pad from which you can access other realms through dimensional travel, open to receive downloads from benevolent forces, and ground these energies and new information into the earth."

Matrina must have read the expression on my face, because she paused and started on a new track.

"This all may sound 'way out there' because it is. It's beyond what we can know. It requires us to open up to experiences that lie beyond the mind. We alter our state of consciousness through sound—at will and on a regular basis—to experience altered states of consciousness, although we have it backwards. Altered states really aren't altered at all. The sleep we walk around in for the majority of our lifetime? Now that's altered! Remember, as I mentioned earlier, we only understand about 3% of our brain's functions. Three percent!"

"I remember you said that before. That's a little spooky. I mean, what on earth is that other 97% capable of?"

"It's natural for fearful feelings to arise when we experience something new and unfamiliar. We're not sure what's happening. Our mind has no way to categorize, slice and dice, and otherwise explain what's going on. It—the mind—doesn't really like that feeling. But it's completely okay. There are no dangers here. You will only ever encounter yourself. While that can still be very challenging, it's always worthwhile. Support is built into the practice. The more you take refuge in the sounds, the easier your shifts will be."

"That's good to know. Should I focus on something in particular?"

"No, not any *thing*. Sure, you'll set your intent and you'll perhaps think thoughts about the practice or notice what's happening in your body, but your focus will be on remaining aware. Your focus is soft and encompassing. This takes practice. It takes practice to let go of mental control, to allow thoughts and ideas to drift through the mind like clouds, especially those niggling little judgmental ones. The more you let go, the more and more you'll find yourself embodying presence and honoring the sounds arising from within you."

"So presence is the focus."

"To satisfy that mind of yours, let's just say, sure! Just as you'll allow movement and thought, it's also important to allow the sound. As I demonstrate or lead you in an exercise, you'll hear my experimental palette being expressed. But remember, you have your own palette."

"Palette?"

"You know: volume, pitch, pitch fluctuation, timbre, how long you sound a tone or how short, how you launch a sound — all of that. There's more to it, of course, but that's all you need to know for now. Part of this work is learning to sense where you are and where you want to go—not you the mind, but you the Being. So if I'm singing an *EE* on a low note, and you are just dying to soar, go for it! If I'm toning a bright, sustained *OH*, and you feel utterly compelled to whisper it, honor that impulse. If it doesn't feel right once you've done it, you can come back to match me. You can only know by doing, by trying, by modifying."

"But I need to at least stay within the framework you provide, don't I?"

"You do need to spend time learning the pieces of the practice as they're taught. You're laying a foundation that you'll use to integrate the numerous elements into a coordinated whole. You might feel quite uncoordinated and unsure of yourself at first. Eventually, you'll let go and fly free. Trust the process. Trust yourself. Every moment is the moment you've been waiting for."

She watched me for a moment and then continued. "Movement is an important element here too. I'm not speaking of a particular set of movements or a prescribed sequence. The movement arises spontaneously in you as you sound. Allow it. You may find yourself doing some really beautiful and delicate gestures, stretching and dancing, or you may just suddenly feel like standing up or sitting down or weaving and bobbing. This motion will ultimately assist you in navigating the space and time shifts that sound creates. These movements will also help you ground the energies into your body and help you focus. Questions?"

I nodded no.

"Good. I think we're ready to begin."

Matrina taught me a new breathing technique she called "topping off." I began by exhaling to empty my lungs. Then I inhaled through my nose. When I had taken a full breath, I sipped just a little bit more air and held that for as long as I could, but not so long that it got uncomfortable. Right before the pressure became too great, I exhaled.

"For today's practice, let's sit with our backs straight. From this position, feel free to move your arms, legs, or head, but remain sitting. Next, we choose a sound to tone. How about *AH*?"

"Sure."

"Place your hands over the heart; that's where we'll be directing the energy. Placing your hands on an area of your body helps direct your intent as you tone."

"Wait. What's our intent?"

"Let's say our intent is to send some yummy energy to the heart. Now, inhale silently, sounding the tone in your mind. At the top of the inhalation, take in just a little more air, now hold, hold, just long enough to feel pressure build, not long enough to feel nervous, and exhale while toning the sound *AH*."

I let out an embarrassing squeak of a note.

"Don't worry about how the tone sounds. Allow it to express itself; it will evolve as your energy shifts. Sometimes this happens immediately, and sometimes it can take more time than you have available in any one sitting. Just do your best. Use your imagination to visualize the sound coming from your bones and traveling the many channels of your heart center."

As I practiced, I began to actually feel something happening in my chest. A warmth spread, and beneath that, I felt a tightness trying to let go.

"You may want to plug your ears with your fingers or even wear earplugs to feel the vibrational energies as they work within your body."

When I plugged my ears, the tone reverberated inside me even more powerfully, making it easier for me to let go.

We continued this meditation for about 11 minutes. From the very start, I felt hot all over. About halfway through, my wrists felt like they wanted to rotate, so I let them. I loved to tone, but combining toning with meditation felt special...like a communion.

At the end, Matrina instructed me to use the silence to just be and direct the energies that had arisen in my heart toward other parts of my body. I imagined a blossoming lotus, its fragrance and color spreading out within me, and I realized for the first time that the quiet created after toning is even more powerful than the toning itself.

The 9th Gate: True Voice

It occurred to me that up to now, I'd never really heard Matrina sing. I was pretty sure she could, based on what she was teaching me, but wouldn't it be funny if she couldn't carry a tune? Sure, I'd heard her tone, and it sounded as if she had a nice voice, but then, anyone can tone.

I got my chance to find out when Matrina invited me to an engagement where she'd been asked to sing. The event was a consciousness conference of some kind, held in a hotel's banquet room. Everyone wore rainbow nametags and chatted amiably across those big round tables while waiters kept refilling glasses of iced tea.

The speaker that night was interesting enough, sharing the latest studies about the energetics of the heart. He introduced Matrina right before dessert. He told us that he first heard her sing years ago on a retreat in Mexico. He promised that we were all in for a real treat.

There was no musical accompaniment. Not much of an auspicious beginning, I thought. When Matrina stepped up to the mic, she just stood there for an unnerving minute, scanning the room. It was almost as if she had stagefright, which I was pretty sure wasn't possible for a woman dressed in gold lamé and leopard prints. Then she closed her eyes and seemed to pray. People started muttering to each other. When she uttered her very first note, however, everyone...even the waiters...stopped what they were doing. Her singing held us all spellbound. Conversations dropped, servers held their cheesecake trays suspended, and people heading to the exits turned back, all to look at her, stunned by what they were hearing.

Her voice was pure, nothing flashy, but all were dazzled. She captured something ineffable. When she finished, not one person applauded...at least, not at first. Oh, that silence was unlike anything I'd ever experienced in my entire life. It was so vast, I just wanted to wallow in it forever. Then one person broke the spell with a clap, and soon everyone followed suit until the room was engulfed in an uproar of cheers. How did she do it? I wanted to know. I asked her about it later when we were alone.

"I am a servant of Sacred Sound. I place myself in complete trust when and where I am meant to give this gift. No matter what passes my lips, as long as I'm aware, it becomes a prayer. Each syllable—each tone—is imparted with intent to heal, inspire, and evolve those in its presence. With awareness, even *hello* or *no thank you* become passages to enlightenment. With my voice, I open channels—new channels, not those deeply rutted and entrenched channels that you've been taught are the only channels. No, my voice embodies all possibility. It's beyond observation and can only be experienced in each moment. My voice is as unique as a fingerprint. I don't try to sound like anybody else or impress people. In my voice is a life—Life itself. My voice—and yours too—is a living being, a pulsing form directly linked to the Divine. When I allow that divinity to flow, I am no longer Matrina. I am immersed, One with the Creator. I sing it all into being."

I'd listened to her speak to me for all those months I'd known her, and I'd only now heard her sing. I knew whatever she said was true. She embodied a mystery that I could no longer doubt. In that moment, I realized I completely trusted Matrina. That's something I hadn't felt toward anyone in a very long time. It shook me to my core. Did I truly appreciate what I was learning? Was I dedicated enough? Could I ever live up to these teachings? I wanted to be worthy. Whatever this was, whatever *she* was, I resolved to take it very seriously.

"Where did *you* learn to sing?" she asked, redirecting me from my deep thoughts.

"I think Joni Mitchell taught me to sing with her *Court & Spark* album."

"No doubt she influenced you. But you don't sound like Joni Mitchell when you sing. How did you learn to sing like you?"

"I don't know. I never thought about it."

"Time to change that."

The following night, Matrina took me to an open mic, where we sat and listened to several different performers, including a young guitar player who covered a Jack Johnson song.

"What do you think of him?" Matrina asked me.

"He's good. He sounds just like Jack Johnson. But...I don't know. There's nothing really there."

"Astute. He *isn't* Jack Johnson, so no one is really hearing Jack Johnson. At the same time, since he isn't singing in his own voice, no one else is singing either."

"So what exactly are we hearing then, and who on earth is singing?"

"No one really. It sounds good, but it has no presence. It's sterile."

The audience clapped when Jack-not-Jack completed his number. Then a young woman with a guitar took the stage. She sang a Rickie Lee Jones cover. She didn't sound anything like Rickie Lee Jones, though. In fact, her voice was quite different and her cover unique.

"Wow, she's really good, isn't she? She has presence. She's singing in her own voice, too."

"Yes. You can hear and feel the difference it makes. Don't get me wrong. I mean, there are some artists so skilled at copying, they make their living doing it. It takes a certain talent to copy well. And copying is a great way to learn—the way you did listening to Joni."

"I think I understand now. Thankfully, I kept learning and developing my own style. I didn't try to be another Joni Mitchell."

"We're all born with the gift of our own song. If we fail to exercise this aspect of ourselves, we become copycats and our gift ends there. We may sound good, but there's no life in the sound. If we draw only from what we know to be safe or acceptable, we lose our capacity to be present. We deprive the world of our unique timbre."

"Wow, I never really thought about that before."

"We can either copy something or improve upon it. But I can take you even further. I'm going to show you something that will teach you to listen more fully to hear what's coming and to know what's needed. I'll show you a form of improvisation that's a tool for developing wisdom—not just in singing, but in all areas of life. It can teach you to trust yourself and your creative impulses—to break out of artistic mediocrity and break through membranes of your potential."

"When do we start?"

"Tomorrow. As you learn to do this with your music, you'll begin to transfer this ability to other areas of your life. You'll become more fluid in all situations, able to create spontaneously amidst your challenges and in cooperation with others. You'll begin to hear the music of life and assert your harmonies within it."

"It sounds incredible. I can't wait."

෨ ෪

The next day, Matrina had me watch an online video of Bobby McFerrin. I was so excited watching what that man is able to do with his voice just off the cuff.

"He's so amazing! How does he do it?"

"I was hoping you wanted to know how *you* can do it."

"Er, that's what I meant to say."

"Well, I want you to apply everything you've learned so far. Begin just by listening."

"Listening to what? The video?"

"No. Just to what you hear right now."

I closed my eyes and listened. "I hear the trees rustling in the breeze. I hear my refrigerator humming. I hear birds...cardinals, I think."

"Perfect. Sing it!"

"Sing what?"

"Sing what you hear or sing along with what you hear. Don't think, just do it."

So I began to make some sounds. First, I blew my breath along with the trees. Then I added a little humming sound in a harmonious pitch with the fridge. I then chirped at rhythmically appointed times. I felt ridiculous at first, unsure of myself, but it slowly became playful and fun.

"That's just one way to learn to improvise. It's easy; anybody can do it. You don't need to be a musician, or should I say: you don't need to think you are one. You do, however, have to be willing to play like a child. Here's another way." Matrina made a very fun sound: a cross between a frog and a record scratch. She kept it up in time. When I got the hang of her groove, I added a new *OH-OH* sound to the mix. I couldn't believe it was that simple.

"See how easy it is? You just pay attention. You feel. And you jump in. It's a lot like being on a high diving board, ice-cold water below. You just have to go for it. Once you jump, the only way is down. Once you're falling, you can't help but find your wings."

We tried another one. This time I started with a sound...a sort of *OOOGA-SWISH*. Matrina came in with *A DO DEE TAH*. It started out okay, but we soon crashed, laughing.

"It's okay to make mistakes," she said putting the word *mistakes* in air quotes. "You've got to be willing to take risks to discover new things. Let's try that one again." So we returned to our *OOOGA SWISH* improvisation. This time, we were better able to follow each other using body language to hint at our direction. It was great fun.

"Once you get comfortable taking risks, then you can work

quite deeply and magically. You can tune into voices of different periods of time, various groups, or even objects and voice improvisations on their behalf."

"What do you mean?"

"Well, you could begin with a meditation that takes you into the oppressed voices of slaves rising in protest. Or you can voice the sounds of children at play. Tune into a cheering crowd or a group of praying monks. Sing a song for peace, a song for the ocean, a song for your liver, or a song of gratitude. There's really no limit. As far as your imagination can reach, that's where your voice can carry you."

It was a fascinating idea. "So, let's say I want to sing a song to my goldfish. I just tune into George and start sounding?"

"Yes. It's simple."

"But how do I know if I'm doing it ri…?" I caught myself and we both laughed. "Right. Sorry. There is no *right* way, and therefore, no wrong way."

"Just have fun," Matrina said. "Sometimes, these soundings will take you very deep, into mysterious experiences you can barely describe. Sometimes, they'll be light and fun and little else. But allow yourself the joy of simply creating in the moment."

ॐ ॐ

When I got home from work the next day, Matrina was sitting on the floor in my living room listening to my CD of Tibetan monks chanting. Her eyes were closed and her breathing was very deep and slow. I was afraid to disturb her, as she seemed deep in meditation.

After I put my things away and sat down next to her, she opened her eyes.

"Ready to learn a mantra?"

"Okay, sure."

"Mantras have been gaining recognition in the West in part due to the popularity of yoga. How would you define the word?"

"Sacred words or sounds that one repeats over and over again?"

"Not bad. Mantras are also accelerants, charmed syllables that 'make the fire hotter,' so to speak. They each have their own unique qualities to affect the body, mind, and spirit in various ways. They can even purify our environment. The Tibetans believe that toning and chanting are tools for enlightenment that awaken the *inner sound*. Practitioners spend their lifetimes repeating mantras over and over, learning to resonate their bodies with these sacred sounds."

"Hundreds and thousands of times, right?"

"Yes. Just imagine how, through the theory of *Eternal Fade*, the sounds of the repeated mantras resound throughout eternity. The Tibetan practitioner is perpetually wrapped in a sacred sound bubble; in other words, he's less likely to be unconsciously entrained to something undesirable." She paused to turn off the CD. "In the tradition of Tantric Yoga, mantras are used for healing, paralyzing, attracting, unbalancing, controlling, changing, opposing, or expanding."

"Did you say paralyzing?"

She ignored the question in her way, which by now I knew meant it was irrelevant to our conversation.

"When you chant, you should hear the mantra in your mind as you inhale. When you breathe out, you speak or sing the mantra. Got it? So I'm going to give you a mantra, and it essential you say it exactly as I give it to you. Do not vary the phrasing, pitch, or pronunciation. I'd like you to work with this mantra over the next week, twice a day. Repeat it 108 times during each session."

"Why 108 times?"

"It's a sacred number to the Yungdrung Bon and in other cultures of the East. There are said to be 108 lies that humans tell, as well as 108 forms of ignorance. There are 108 energy lines converging from the heart chakra, and 108 paths to God. There are 108 stages of the soul, oh, and my personal favorite: 54 letters of the Sanskrit alphabet."

"Wait. 54?"

"Each letter has a masculine and a feminine energy, hence 108."

"So twice a day? Should I do it at morning and at night?"

"Don't get stuck in the details."

"Okay, okay. Sorry. What will happen when I repeat this mantra?"

"This is a very special mantra. It will open you in ways that you cannot imagine, but only if you follow directions."

"Right. Without getting stuck in the details, of course," I couldn't help but let that slip out under my breath.

ॐ ॐ

I practiced and practiced that mantra wondering when I'd see Matrina again so we could get back to talking about it. Finally, one afternoon, just as I'd taken a seat on the couch to read a book, Matrina came into the room. "Ready to work with the mantra?"

"Hi. Yes, I think I have it down!"

"Let's hear it."

So I began reciting the mantra. I was very careful to say it with precision. All of my energy and focus was directed toward the proper pronunciation and timing.

"That's not bad. Very precise. But you aren't saying it fast enough. Try saying it faster. Work with it some more. We'll revisit it next week."

Another week passed, and Matrina finally reappeared. She asked me to repeat the mantra. I began slowly and then sped it up.

"Not fast enough. Faster! Faster!"

In my effort, I was losing the phrasing, the articulation, and pronunciation. It was coming out all wrong, and I had to steer myself back with concentration to say it properly.

"Yes, yes, very proper, but not fast enough. Come on!"

She was pushing me, and I was getting irritated. I was saying it as fast as I could. Then she said, "Let go of doing it right!" and something magical happened. I let go of the mantra, and I could actually feel the right side of my brain taking control. Sounds were flying out of my mouth that held little resemblance to the mantra, but at the same time, some energy had taken over. It was powerful. I was speaking nonsense with an uninhibited joy. Tears streamed down my face.

When I finished, Matrina looked at me and smiled. "Well, that was amazing! See what happens when we stop trying to 'do it right?' Life takes over."

"What was that? I mean, what just happened? I wasn't even saying the mantra!"

"I just told you. You let Life take over. You weren't saying the mantra because you *became* Mantra. You gave command of your ship to the part of you that doesn't think. You discovered a language that comes from the soul. You practiced something to the point of mastery, and then you let it go. So often, we master things and hold on to them for dear life. We never get to discover the undiscovered within the mastery. Today, you broke through to the back side of mastery, where the power of creation lies. You surrendered to what is."

Most of what she had just said made sense then and there. The rest would surely come.

"How does it feel?" she asked, watching me.

"Awesome. And kind of scary too. I mean, I can't quite understand with my mind what just happened and if it was okay. It almost felt like I was going crazy."

Matrina laughed. "No, you're not going crazy. If anything, you're discovering your sanity, and that just *feels* crazy."

"It reminds me of something I've heard that happens in Pentecostal churches. I don't know much about it, but they have a practice of speaking in tongues. It's supposed to be the Holy Spirit."

"Speaking in tongues—otherwise known as *glossolalia*—has its roots in ancient tribal and religious practices. The idea is to let go, sometimes into a trance-like state, and allow Spirit to speak through you. Some people who practice glossolalia later translate it into understandable spiritual messages."

"Are you telling me that the gibberish I just spouted actually meant something?"

"Well, sure. Why not? The only thing that makes the words I'm speaking to you now mean what they mean is our agreement that they mean what they mean. Without that agreement, they'd be gibberish too. You don't speak Swahili, right? If you heard it, you might think it was nonsense, but it has meaning to those who have agreed what the meaning is. Yes?"

"I understand. But the implication is that there's no more substance to a language than what we've decided. I mean, maybe that's obvious, but I never thought about it. I just always assumed that 'apple' meant the red fruit growing on the tree because that's what an apple is. Wow, we talked about this at the very beginning, didn't we?"

"You've just made an important connection. If you started calling an apple a *plepo*, people might either think you were nuts or from another country. But if they agreed that the thing hanging from the branch was a plepo, then that's what it would become to everyone."

"I feel confusion setting in."

"We can use that. In fact, glossolalia can help you to express and make sense of that confusion. There's a science behind what's happening, but we don't need to go into that too deeply right now. Just know that glossolalia lights up a part of the brain that's better equipped to surrender to your confusion. It helps you let go when your habit would've been to reason and control everything."

"I did kind of feel ridiculous at first. It was uncomfortable and sounded just plain silly." I watched that glow appear around Matrina and knew what was coming.

"Once you got over yourself and the embarrassment of making strange sounds, you were able to get in touch with a part of you that's comfortable with and open to mystery. The point is to accept what the practice of making gibberish did for you. Can you allow it to provide you with a rich resource for inner guidance that bypasses your judging, justifying, 'need-to-know' mind? That's the ten million dollar question."

She watched me as my mind sped through a series of gear shifts.

"The ether, the Akashic records, the *Nagual*. By any name, we're talking about containers of all knowledge. This information is being sent to the human race like never before; it's the key to a mass awakening. The spontaneous arising of psychic abilities, the reception of high frequencies, and more—all are information 'deliveries,' if you will. This multidimensional information is being received by receptive humans, whether or not they have the capacity to recognize the gift. Even those who are aware that something extraordinary is happening don't necessarily know what to do with it.

"One of the best ways to bring the information out into the world is through the technique of speaking in tongues or glosso-lalia. Speaking in tongues bypasses the rational, reasoning mind—as well as the restraints of our language—allowing the purest energy of the information to be expressed. We are the vehicles through which information from the higher realms is made manifest upon earth. For example, let's consider crop circles."

"Crop circles?" I was incredulous.

"Hear me out. The human mind tends to ask, 'How did this

occur? What is this? What does it mean? Is it man-made or miracle, hoax or credible?' If we were to forget our need to know the answers to those questions for the moment and focus instead on the energy that such a symbol is meant to convey—if we learned to listen with our ears wide open—we'd begin to hear the message. We could then surrender to that message and bring it forth in glossolalia. But speaking in tongues, while sufficient to disseminate energy, is not quite enough to share the meaningful nuggets that the sounds represent. So once we master the art of glossolalia, we must then turn our attention to interpreting it into language. This translation of our speaking in tongues must be done from the heart center, not from the mind."

"So...then...what did I just say?"

"Good question, child. Close your eyes, go deep, and answer it for yourself."

I did just that. I closed my eyes and focused on my breathing until I reached a very relaxed state. Then I asked myself what the message was. I began speaking out loud, "I am the center of the circle. I am the center of the spiral that coils up to Heaven and plunges to the Underworld. I am the space between all things. I am the rhythm of the beating of wings. I am the fire in the lion's dreams. So awaken and treat everything as sacred, live in gratitude constantly, and follow intuition. Only through mastering intent and surrendering to creative impulse can we break down our resistances to miracles. Karma is the veil that prevents us from seeing the truth, from spontaneously healing, from performing miracles. But all is already forgiven. It is merely up to you to accept it."

Wow. I had the ability to rant just like Matrina.

ℰℬ ℭℛ

Since meeting Matrina, I'd come to understand that claiming a deep sense of freedom of expression was indeed the warrior's path. Nothing about this work was easy, although it offered plenty of rewards. It was a constant challenge to question and open, to release and expand.

Before meeting Matrina, I was frustrated about my singing. Now I was slowly and gratefully overcoming my performance blocks and finding more opportunities to sing and record. I had to feel the fear and do it anyway, so to speak.

As always, Matrina picked up on my train of thought. "Wrenne, what makes a great performer great?"

"Do you mean great as in popular?"

"Great question! No, I mean great as in riveting and magical. I'd love to hear what you think about that."

"Hmm...I'm not sure. I guess they are authentic...you know, not being Jack-not-Jacks."

"Okay. Good. What else?"

"I think great performers have to love what they do."

"Yes, absolutely. And?"

"And I suppose there is a professionalism, a polish."

Matrina made a buzzer sound. "Sorry, you didn't win the prize behind door number three. Time for a field trip."

Matrina took me downtown. It was a warm summer night with a cool breeze in the air...perfect busking weather. As usual, several musicians had set up along the sidewalks, keeping a respectful distance from one another.

While walking toward the buskers, we passed a snazzy nightclub where some cool jazz flowed out the doorway. We stopped to listen. The band was very professional; they wore nice suits, and the vocalist wore a slinky red dress and heels. People drank cocktails and talked over the music, although some were attentive to the performance.

"Is she a great performer?"

"She's good. I like her voice. But I wouldn't say she was great."

"She's polished, though?"

"Yes, and maybe that's it. It's a little too polished."

We continued on. Turning the corner onto a side street, we came upon a drummer and guitarist. The drummer danced as he played.

"Are these two great performers?"

"Absolutely."

"Do they have polish?"

"Well, no, not like that jazz band. But they have a guitar case full of fives and tens and a rapt audience. And they have something else…they are full of life, aren't they?"

"Now you know what makes a great performer great."

"What, life?"

"Yes. They are in the moment, totally carried away by the music, but completely aware of the multidimensions of their performance."

"Um…care to elaborate?"

"Performing is a multidimensional event. There's the external dimension where everything is about the crowd, the environment, your band mates, your voice teachers, all that external validation. It's neither good nor bad, positive nor negative. But if it's your sole focus, your performance is out of balance and inauthentic. Jack-not-Jack. Then there's the internal dimension. There are of course many excellent performers who operate from this level, where the focus is on the energy of the self: your physical being, your emotions, your phrasing, and your actual voice.

"It's obvious why this tends to be the dimension we're most aware of as singers. But if we get stuck there, the imbalance can result in a sense of self-importance, and we lose our fluidity. Like our jazz lady in the red dress. The dimension that's often lacking or unacknowledged is the one that adds greater depth to what we bring to our performances. It is the dimension of the secret realm."

"Secret realm? You've mentioned that before, but I still don't understand it."

"I'm using the word *secret* here as the Buddhists do—to mean hidden. It's secret because it's remained out of our tangible reality for so long that it's often dismissed or ignored. On this level, the focus becomes the energy of spirit, the meaning beyond the lyrics, our connection to other, our presence and light, and turning to something bigger than self. This level must be grounded by the other two—the internal and external dimensions—or we lack substance."

"The drummer and guitar player had that?"

"Whether they realized it or not, they were in touch with it, yes. It's only in moving fluidly though and between each dimension that we become whole performers—balanced, riveting, and magical. It's a practice that can be cultivated with our awareness and the conscious consideration we're willing to give to our singing."

"How do I put all this together? How do I use it?"

"Much of the work we've done together has been for the sole—or soul—purpose of reclaiming your faith. First, we worked with letters and words to cleanse your will—your intent. What we covered about sound, the voice, and toning now comprises your toolbox. When you pull out one of these tools with your pure intent, that's where the magic begins."

The 10th Gate: Rainbow Light

It was every singer's nightmare: I had lost my voice. I thought this would put my work with Matrina on hold, but using the moment as she does, she began sharing with me the importance of caring for the voice.

"It's important to know the signs of vocal fatigue or injury. The voice is incredibly resilient—even when we overdo it, but there are things we can do to take better care of it. Even just one day of silence can do wonders for our stressed out larynx and chords. How do you know when you may be making a sound that hurts your vocal chords?"

"When something doesn't feel right," I croaked.

"Don't talk, for God's sake!" She chastised me.

"Then don't ask a question," I whispered.

"Fair enough. But don't even whisper; that just makes it worse. You're better off sounding all scratchy than trying to whisper." She handed me a writing tablet and pen. "The best thing is some silence—a real break from speaking and singing. The thing is, some of the warning signs of overwork can also be good signs—signs that energy is moving in new ways. So you really have to pay attention."

I wrote, "I don't get it."

"For example, coughing a lot can mean you're doing something wrong or that you've just managed to clear a very big block of energy in your fifth chakra. Generally, though, tickling, coughing, pinching, irritation, tightening, or having to reach for a sound—those are all warning signs to ease up."

I scribbled as fast as I could, "I admit I don't always pay attention to those things. I just plow through them."

"Well, as a performer, you've learned to do that, but when you're just learning to tone, you don't have to control your sounds. You may want to 'do it right' or give a certain impression, but that can lead to bad habits and injury."

"Maybe I'm coming down with something," I wrote.

"Are you experiencing any nasal congestion?"

I shook my head no.

"I think something else is going on. While I'm on the subject, if you ever do get congested, try clearing your nasal passages with the sounds *HUM*, *NNN*, and *MA*. You can do this in the shower for the added benefit of the steam. Here. Let me show you something called the *Shankh Mudras*, which is a hand yoga position for the throat. It nourishes the throat center. You can do it while in silent meditation or while toning."

Matrina removed the pen and paper from my grip and took hold of my hands. "To form it, put up your hands like you are singing, 'Stop—in the name of love.' Now grab your left thumb with your right hand, right thumb extended upward. Keep the fingers of your left hand together as you bring your right thumb and left fingers together."

My right thumb met the middle finger of my left hand, forming a shape like a conch shell. I held this position at throat level, keeping my awareness on my throat. It felt good.

"Hold that. Now then, let's talk about what's really going on with that lost voice of yours."

I looked at her questioningly.

"Well, there's the physical apparatus, but there's also the psychological aspect of the voice. What's going on that you don't have a voice? What are you afraid of saying?"

Dropping the mudra, I picked up the pen and pad, suddenly feeling blind to the obvious. "Actually, I was asked to present some of my poetry in two weeks. I said yes, and now I'm starting to feel really nervous about it. I've never been part of a poetry reading before. Do you think that's what this is all about?"

"That makes sense. But don't worry. You're a performer. You'll be fine."

I scribbled in an urgent hand, "But Matrina, the poetry I want to share, it's so personal and close to my heart! I've never shared it with anyone!"

"Ah, I see."

"Advice?" I squeaked.

She gave me a stern, motherly look. "Shush!" With that, she placed her hands at my throat. Her lips moved, but I couldn't tell what she was saying. I felt a twitching sensation and saw a shimmery turquoise light behind my eyes. Gradually, a malaise took over, making me feel drowsy. I must have fallen asleep then and there because I had a dream.

I stood on the balcony in the rotunda of a government building that overlooked the floor below. The place was packed with people, both downstairs and with me on the balcony. As we watched from above, a small crowd was antagonizing one individual. The scene abhorred me. Not one person spoke up on behalf of the individual. The pressure in me began to build as my mind went through all the fears of being the sole voice of reason in such a large crowd. If I spoke up, would anyone even hear me? And if they did, would they then descend upon me as well?

In a flash, I no longer cared; I *had* to say something. I opened my mouth. At first, nothing came out. Then a small "Stop!" escaped. I repeated the word, adding, "This isn't right." Like a wave, my voice carried out over the crowd.

At first, people just looked at me dumbfounded, unsure how to respond. Then they waited to see how the rest of the crowd would respond. Nothing happened. They all turned away and back to the horror below.

I became bolder and more persistent. More and more people listened. And then, as I found my voice and expressed myself without doubt, everyone began to really see what was happening, as if waking from a dream. Soon, my voice was joined by others...

When I woke up, my voice was back. It turned out I wasn't coming down with anything, nor had I overdone it. Matrina later explained that I simply had an energy block working its way out of my throat center.

"Dreams are perhaps the best place to work through such blocks. Your dreaming self was able to give you a clear affirmation that you were ready to release your fears and speak your power. And then—pop!"

"The block is gone."

"Here. I brought you something to wear at your poetry debut." Matrina handed me a gorgeous Navajo turquoise necklace.

"Oh, Matrina! It's beautiful! Thank you!"

"Turquoise is a powerful protector that will remind you of the spiritual nature of your voice. It enhances communication."

"I've heard that gemstones have different healing properties. I thought maybe it was just superstition."

"They work the same way any vibrational tool does—through resonance and entrainment. Each gemstone carries a unique vibration, different from every other gemstone. If you have ears to hear it, you can even hear gemstones singing."

"Stones sing?"

"That's right. For example, smoky quartz has a very low crackly voice. It is a very powerful purifier that transmutes negativity. Citrine, on the other hand, is great for clearing the mind and stabilizing the emotions. Its voice is very smooth and clear."

"What about this?" I grabbed a quartz crystal off of my desk.

"Nice. Quartz is an amplifier. I suggest you try toning with this one sometime. It'll help you deepen your meditation."

Before handing it back to me, Matrina held my quartz inside both her hands and closed her eyes. She seemed to be praying over it. Then she took an inhalation, and raising her hands to her lips, she blew sharply into the stone.

"What was that for?"

"Just a little magic. Quartz is like a computer. It can hold a great deal of information. I told this one some secrets for later."

That made me smile. "Here. Help me put this on," I said, handing her the necklace. Then I went to the mirror to see it.

"Gosh, Matrina. This is really special. Thank you!"

"You are so welcome, child. Now, go boldly and share your truth."

ℬ ℭℛ

Matrina always wore such gorgeous colors. With her dark skin, she looked wonderful in bold and bright hues that I didn't think I could wear. But lately, since she had taught me the technique for breathing in color, I felt myself drawn more powerfully by colors in my environment. I found myself shopping for brighter clothes at the store and wearing more colors. Then I bought some pastels and paper for the first time since I was a kid and began experimenting to create colorful abstracts. I even painted my walls. I just wanted to be awash with color.

Matrina told me that the more we work with color, the more we see the relationship between color and sound. In fact, she said, many people see colors when they tone. Since I've had experiences of *hearing* colors, I knew she was probably right. Colors are really sounds and vice versa. They are also tools that can lend energy to our healing work.

I knew, for example, that each chakra of the body was often associated with a particular color, a spectrum of experience, and a tone. I'd known about chakras before working with Matrina, of course, which was helpful since she'd sometimes refer to them when we worked together. What still confused me was that different sources cited different associations. Was the color of the crown chakra purple or gold or white? Was the sound for the root chakra *OO* or *LAM* or *DZA*? Who was right? It was a question that came up for me again and again.

When I asked Matrina to clarify, she laughed and said my

favorite word was *right*. Then she explained, "In different books, you'll find different authors proclaiming different tones, colors, and syllables to represent the different chakras. We've talked about this before. Suffice it to say that there is no *right* answer. There is validity in every tradition. You must always honor any author's inner knowing and then develop an inner knowing of your own."

"But why is there discrepancy?"

"There's more than one reason. In most courses on the chakra system, instruction focuses on each of the seven main chakras, their respective emotional charges, colors, gemstone and tone corollaries, etc. That information is very useful, and for those who have never spent time learning about and working with chakras, it's an essential and highly recommended step on their, or anyone's, journey."

When she explained it like that, it seemed obvious.

She continued. "It's important to cleanse and purify what's there. A great deal of energy and information can be gained by doing this. At some point, though, it becomes important to move beyond our present knowledge of what the chakras are and how they work. Our DNA is changing quite rapidly. What was once true for the human race for thousands of years is now no longer relevant for everyone. There just isn't one right way anymore."

"There is no one right way. There is no one right way," I repeated to myself in the hopes it would finally sink in.

"Typically, people are always trying to balance and expand their chakras, widening them in the front and the back in order to take in more information. There's a belief that our chakras become blocked or clogged, and while at one level that's certainly true, the limitation is in concluding that the ultimate result of any healing practice is a fully opened, balanced chakra. That's a bit of a misconception. It's like settling for an aspirin to quell your headaches rather than finding a way to live a life free of headaches. If we were truly healed and whole, we wouldn't even have chakras."

"Get out of here!" I couldn't believe it. But the thought resonated with me and rooted itself deep within me. Now I understand that the visual images I held while working with my chakra system for so many years had held me back, preventing me from growing into the next phase of development. I held my chakras in isolation...one, two, three, etc.

Matrina gave me a moment to process what she'd said and then took it a step further. "The chakra system as we know it is comprised of separate, open energy centers, but our natural state is like one big chakra. It is the Rainbow Light Body written about in Buddhism. A handful of lamas have been known to achieve it, usually at death. Achieving the Rainbow Light Body occurs for masters upon death because that's when the illusion of dualism is finally dispelled; that's the moment the elemental energies comprising the physical body are released back into the primordial essence. Our goal now, in life rather than in death, is to achieve the Rainbow Light Body by dissolving the boundaries of our chakras and learning to radiate from our core out, as one sun with light in our veins. Merging the chakras creates a subtle light body that we can learn to develop and control."

"Sounds unbelievable. So the question is, how do we do that? We've spent so much time learning how to strengthen our chakras, how to individuate them, how to work with them one by one. Now what?"

"First, let me just say that beliefs about the chakra system are deeply entrenched. Some people may find my words threatening, so don't go blabbing this information to everyone."

"Rats! I was just thinking of all the people I can't wait to tell. They'll flip!"

"I assure you, the traditional ideas and ways of working with the chakras are still valid and useful. Especially for those in the healing arts. Don't rock any boats unnecessarily. They may try to explain away these ideas using fear-based images of alien implants and supernatural energy drainage. I'm happy to say the chakras weren't designed by some extraterrestrial race with a desire to feed off of and control our energetic states."

"I'm certainly glad to hear that," I said raising an eyebrow and wondering who might have thought that about chakras.

"Chakras are a necessary filtering device for what would otherwise have been an overwhelming, circuit-frying energetic capacity."

"You mean, now we're ready to access that capacity?"

"With a great deal of preparation, yes. We have to cultivate a certain level of awareness first; take a certain level of personal responsibility; and make sure to put in place certain understandings. It's the journey of the spiritual warrior. We must be beyond believing the perceptions of our limited senses. Once we're less restricted by that, we can finally begin to remove the protective filtering system of our chakras from our DNA."

"It sounds like we'll be able to take in more and more information, have a greater access to everything."

"Sound plays an essential role in this process. The Rainbow Light Body has been described as the highest rate of vibratory form. It can also be described as alignment with Truth embodied. We must be both very care-ful and care-free in using words. We must wield our unique vibration with pureness and clarity. We must love ourselves unconditionally, while at the same time accepting the vaporous truth of our nonexistence. We must open to Life and be consumed by it."

"I'm beginning to understand something."

"What's that?"

"Paradox really is okay. I'm beginning to see that all people are living their own dream in their own universe. Just because I get an intuitive hit about something doesn't mean it's true for other people, but it also doesn't mean I'm wrong. The best I can do is to ask for a reflection. It may or may not be confirmed. If it isn't, we can both be right, within our own dreams."

Matrina smiled at me so lovingly, I couldn't help but cry.

"Honey," she said, "for you, that's a major revelation. Now you can serve Sound as a healer. Now we can play in the field beyond right and wrong."

That's when Matrina taught me something she called *Shamanic Voicework*. It was a lot like Vocal Toning Meditation, but it went even deeper. In this process, she had me sit up straight in a cross-legged position, inhale, take a little more breath on the top, and hold it, just like in VTM. But this time, as I held the breath, she told me to imagine the breath as a ball that rose and fell along my spine, settling at a particular chakra. There it acted like a sponge, collecting the unexpressed. Then, when I couldn't hold my breath anymore, I could release a sound on the breath.

I thankfully stopped myself from asking, "What sound?"

"Try to allow the sound its own life," Matrina explained. "Don't censor it with your mind."

I tried it once.

"Not bad, but you shortened its life. Try again and allow the sound to end naturally."

After my next attempt, she said, "Don't cut it off. Go right into another one."

I repeated the process.

"Ah, that was more authentic. Good. This time, before you even make the sound, really listen to it with your inner ear as it arises. Do your best to honor it."

I tried again. She had me cycling through repetitions in threes. In the beginning, the sounds were tight and unfulfilling. Eventually, the sounds coming out were free and expansive. The satisfaction I felt with the last ones made me feel as though I could fly!

Matrina left me to it. I repeated the practice every day for over a month, working through each of the chakras and clearing them with this technique. Some days, I'd reach that satisfaction point quickly. Other times, however, I seemed to have a lot to work through. I always felt some release by the end of the session. With dedication, Matrina said one day I'd be able to express the Rainbow Light Body through this practice.

Meanwhile, I heard from others that my singing voice was maturing and becoming more resonant. I'd also noticed that I wasn't afraid to speak up when necessary, and I was enjoying new and deeper forms of creative expression in my life. Things seemed to be coming together, the work I was to share becoming evident.

PART IV

BEYOND THE GATES

Music runs like blood through my veins
the rhythm of the heart pumping a steady oh so cool groove
though maybe sometimes missing a beat
It holds the bottom while the notes of each of my cells rings out
"I am alive! This is my song."

My pores secrete music
My eyes shine with it
My hair grows because of it
I both move and am still with music
My entire life is a composition of rests and notes
flats, sharps, and naturals

I play so many instruments
my lungs and vocal chords
my mind with thoughts that are sweetly harmonious and
sometimes jarring
That's the one I'd like to master...that mind
this keyboard as I type
dot, dot, dot, t-y-p (beat beat) e
the daughter, the teacher, the healer

Music is Life is Breath is Spirit is God
If I breathe, it is because of music
If I dream, it is because of music
If I love, it is because I AM music

Banging like a drum
Ringing like a bell
Moaning like a cello

I weave through sinews of the harp as I fly

I am music
I am musical
I am music's ally as it is mine

How do we go about so unaware, so deaf?
We are always dancing, but we aren't listening to the beat
we are always singing, but we aren't paying attention to
the lyrics
and sometimes, we aren't bothering to change our tune

I don't want anyone but me determining my melody
I don't want outside influences to dictate my genre
I am an independent label
in the key of absolutely me

Silence

Working with Matrina helped me understand the gift within silence. I'd experienced how powerful the silence was after that toning session, and I felt something I could never hope to express in the silence following her song at the conference. I often sat with Matrina in her own brand of silent meditation, too.

In those meditations, sometimes we didn't even close our eyes, but she never said a damned thing. It unnerved me...we just looked at each other or gazed ahead.

Matrina said that the deepest teachings she could transmit occurred in silence. "Everything else is just mind candy for third-dimensional living."

When we first started these meditations, I felt incredibly awkward, but eventually, I came to love these dreaming states more than anything, a huge gift that taught me the power of presence.

"Silence is the stream of intent. Without silence—without ether and space—there would be only an impenetrable void in which our ability to create would cease to exist. What is a drawing but lines punctuating white space? What is a song but notes filling the emptiness? Silence is also the most powerful form of communication."

"You mean like giving someone the silent treatment can teach them a lesson?"

"I mean that silence is laden with treasures from our soul if we learn to listen well. From silence, all things arise: answers to our questions, sure, but also ideas, wisdom, and melodies. Silence is golden not because it keeps us out of trouble, but because it truly is a precious and invaluable thing. It is our duty to protect it and honor it."

"How?"

"We protect silence when we become more aware of its

opposite—noise. Restaurants with televisions and music compete for our attention over conversations. Machinery and appliances *hum* and *rev* and *whine*, forming a soundtrack to our lives. Constant stimulation tempts us out of the stream of our focused intent into a dream not of our own design."

"Like the TV at the mechanics that time I had my brakes checked."

"Yes. We honor silence when we turn things off! We honor silence when we take just a few moments of our day to breathe, to penetrate nature with our eyes, and to pause. Silence is always present. It just wants a little attention from time to time—a little acknowledgment for all it does for us. As we turn our attention toward silence, it spreads and widens the way the sun burns off clouds in a blue sky. We are treated to a glimmer of our true nature—the vast and still expanse of enlightenment. When sound re-enters, we hear anew, for we begin to understand that silence is within all sounds and all sounds are within silence."

I remembered once being told by an intuitive that my guide was adamantly silent. That kind of pissed me off at the time. I thought, "Oh, great. My celestial guide can't even give me any guidance! What good is a silent guide? Can't see him, can't hear him. What's the point?" I felt cheated.

Only now, after my time with Matrina, do I understand that having a silent guide was the greatest gift I could have ever received. My guide always pointed me to exactly what I needed to remember, realize, and find in any and every moment...silence.

I once asked Matrina if she was my silent guide, thinking maybe she had finally realized the absurdity of keeping silent.

She replied, "Sweetheart, I know you've felt gypped because you have a silent guide. You see, he's taken an eternal vow of silence. But he's always with you, and you have no idea how lucky you are to have him."

She was right. I am lucky. And grateful. Because in my

lifetime, never did I hear any dogma from my guide. Never did I hear a statement that I could misconstrue or misinterpret. Never was I handed strictures or beliefs that complicated or even reinforced the ones I already had. I was never handed anything but an empty bowl that always pointed me back to *THAT*.

ℬ ℭ

After our teachings about silence, Matrina started coming around less and less often. I could tell that things were about to change, and I felt saddened by her inevitable parting. When she stopped popping in and out of my life, I missed her presence.

Then one day, while hiking along the Blue Ridge Parkway, I saw her luminous bubble approach. In a moment, Matrina was standing before me. She looked so different...younger and almost transparent. She wore a fabric of pale rose that sparkled with iridescence in the sun. Her skin was radiant, her eyes deeper than ever...like pools to eternity. It was almost difficult to look into them and just as difficult not to. We embraced and laughed. Then we spent the next several hours catching up with each other.

Later we discovered a rocky overhang that had an incredible echo if you stood underneath it. We played back and forth with it like children.

"This reminds me of a story," she said.

"I love stories!"

We settled down on the rock face and she began. "A woman and her daughter were climbing the mountain, gathering herbs and medicinal plants. The daughter nearly tripped over a half buried stone as she ran ahead into a hollow. Stubbing her toe, she yelled out in pain, 'Ooowww!!'

"Just then, the daughter heard a cry from the other side of the hollow: 'Ooowww!!'

"Curious, the daughter yelled into the hollow, 'Who's there?'

to which came the reply, 'Who's there?'

"This made the daughter indignant, thinking someone was playing a cruel game. This time, she yelled, 'You are nothing to me!' And the voice answered in kind, 'You are nothing to me!'

"The mother, humored by what she'd heard, caught up with her daughter in the hollow.

"'Daughter,' the woman said, 'Pay attention!' Then the mother yelled, 'You are beautiful!' to which the voice replied, 'You are beautiful!' Then the mother yelled, 'I love you!' and the voice echoed back, 'I love you!'

"The mother explained to her open-mouthed daughter that the voice is known as Echo, but truly it is the Voice of Life. 'Life is a mirror of our thoughts, words, and deeds. If you want to have a friend, be one. If you want compassion, give it. If you desire others to be patient and respectful of you, give your patience and respect to them. This is the law.'"

∞ ∝

As the sun sank low, Matrina began what I knew to be her final goodbye.

"I'm so excited for you, Wrenne. You've bravely walked through every gate and are deeply integrating everything you've learned. You are about to return to that which exists beyond thought. Soon, you'll no longer live life; life will live you. You no longer have to think 'how to' in order to function. Like the beating of your heart and your very breath, action will become involuntary as you surrender to the divine, to the heart. Beautiful creations will be the result. You'll find yourself capable of great things—possible now because you won't be doing them of your own volition. Spirit will be working through you."

She paused to wipe a tear that had formed in the corner of my eye. "Child, your journey is just beginning. My visits have given you new perspectives and tools to help you awaken to the power of your Voice. Now it's up to you to put them into practice and discover what is true for you."

I knew Matrina had been preparing me all along to share what I'd learned from her. Still, somehow, I never thought that day would come. I certainly never imagined my life without her. "Matrina, what should I tell people? What is it we need to understand?"

Her answer astounded me. It felt like what people say happens during an accident…when their entire life flashes before them. It came out of her in a rush of words that flowed over me like a wave. Somehow, she managed to summarize everything she had ever taught me in just a few minutes.

"All of life is sound. Only by returning to sound will we be free of form. The voice is a link to a person's power, like a chord or tether from the unmanifest to the manifest. Sound is a bridge between form and formless. If people can learn to walk that bridge between worlds, they will manifest their creations with impeccability. They need to know that sound is love and love is sound. Sound is being. All of life sings and all of life must sing to be healed.

"Tell them their hearts are made of music. From the time they're conceived, they are musical. Tell them that colors and words—all are a form of music, a form of sound. Each person, each living thing, is a vessel of sound—each a unique melody. Sound is a palace in which God resides. Sound is a chalice of awakening: The Holy Grail. The voice is an open vessel for the word of God. Each human is that God, creating his reality through his words. Tell them that the word was our way into creation, and it is our return home. Tell them that every note that's played within the body of a human being is a note that rings through eternity, creating the great *Nada* or All.

"Explain that ancient places are filled with sound; their stones retain wisdom through sound, and with sound, we will reclaim the lost wisdom and knowledge. Explain that sound builds and destroys. Sound is God. All of life is the vibration of creation. We must learn to vibrate at increasingly higher velocities if we are to evolve. We cannot continue to take for granted the power of the word if we are to evolve. We cannot take the power of sound for granted, and we can no longer remain ignorant of the power of music to program us.

"I really must be going. So take heed. Return to sound. Reclaim the art of sound. Learn to listen with our hearts' ears wide open. Learn to listen once more with the entire body as we did before our birth. Allow our words to arise from nothing rather than knowledge, practice, and habit. Break the backs of the symbols that hold us hostage. Turn our vulnerabilities inside out and let them become our power.

"Allow. Surrender. God will speak through you. God will sing through you. And every utterance will heal nations."

Author's Note

The toning circles written about in this book are real, and I'd like to invite you to take part in them. Vocal toning is a Way. As Matrina said, we are just beginning to reclaim the power that awaits us in group toning. Using our voices to express what is inside, beyond words, beyond stories, is a simple practice that helps us come into stillness. Like meditation, tai chi, yoga, or any practice that takes a certain amount of effort and self-discipline, toning can help us feel more centered, more awake, more joyful, and more at peace.

I welcome any reader interested in starting a Toning for Peace Circle to download the Toning for Peace Circle Host packet and application available for free at ToningforPeace.com. Anyone, anywhere can become a Toning for Peace Circle Host. The only thing that is required is interest, a willingness to use the voice freely, and a desire to provide a safe space for others to explore sounding. Those wanting to delve deeper may train to become a Certified Vocal Toning Meditation Facilitator or Practitioner. Additional information is available on the website.

May we all cultivate peace within so we may truly influence peace on the planet.

A-ho! Namaskar!

About the Author

Dielle Ciesco specializes in the transformational power of the voice to heal and connect us with our own Divinity. She is passionate about every Voice, be it the one we use everyday to communicate, the ones we hear inside our heads, the silent voice of wisdom, voices raised in song, or the ones that call us to awaken. The creator of Vocal Toning Meditation, Shamanic Voicework, and Toning for Peace, she is also a DNAvatar, CyberShamanic Dance Wave host, and a featured vocalist on the TLC series with Visionary Music, creators of DNA activation music. With over 18 years experience as a performer, teacher and healing facilitator, Dielle blends her experiences in vocal toning, sacred sound, meditation, Toltec & Bon shamanism, multidimensional music, Reiki Tummo, coaching, and teaching to assist clients in discovering a deeper connection to their inner truth and wisdom. She teaches workshops, writes, sings, makes art, and works one-on-one with clients. This is her first book.

VISIT THE WEBSITES:

TheUnknownMother.com
ToningforPeace.com

CONTACT DIELLE:
dielle@theunknownmother.com

Roundfire Books put simply, publish great stories. Whether it's literary or popular, a gentle tale or a pulsating thriller, the connecting theme in all Roundfire fiction titles is that once you pick them up you won't want to put them down.